THE TOFF AND THE TRIP-TRIP-TRIPLETS

He actually led the way into the lighted patch; anyone glancing this way could see them, but getting across only took seconds. Rollison reached the shadows in a porch overlooking the front door, and as he did so he swivelled round, pulled the pistol from his pocket and the poker from his waistband, and said softly:

"What shall it be, Benbow? A bullet in the heart or a slap with a poker on the back of the neck?"

All four stood like men in a trance; all four, facing him, were within arm's reach. Any one of them could fling himself forward and be shot — but if two took the risk at the same moment, there would be little hope for him.

And none of these men was a coward.

N. J. MACKINLAY. TTT

The Toff and the Trip-Trip-Triplets

John Creasey

CORONET BOOKS
Hodder Paperbacks Ltd., London

CONTENTS

CHAPTER I

Call for Help

"T-T-Toff," the girl breathed into the telephone. "Can you p-p-please come and help me?"

There was such a note of pleading in her voice and such an air of helplessness in her stammer that it was all the Honorable Richard Rollison could do to refrain from saying 'yes' immediately. But there were reasons for caution. In the first place it was three o'clock on a winter's morning, dark as pitch and cold as charity. For another, he did not know who was calling, for she had made the appeal as soon as he had placed the telephone at his lips and announced, voice vague with sleep, that he was Richard Rollison.

Before he responded the girl continued to plead: "*Please. Please* come and help me!"

By now at least he was wide awake and hitching himself up in his double bed. And the door of his room opened to admit his man, Jolly, who looked both dyspeptic and despairing, and quite, quite old. Methuselah old. But when the Toff cocked a thumb towards him he moved with celerity towards an extension telephone at which he could listen in.

"Please—" the girl began again, and then as if with a flare of alarm: "Are you st-st-still there?"

"Yes, I'm here," soothed Rollison.

"Thank g-g-gosh for that!"

"Thank who?" asked Rollison, incredulous about a

'gosh' in the mini-age.

"Gosh!" she insisted. "T-T-Toff, please come and help me. There's n-n-no one else I can turn to. Absolutely no one else."

"Where are you?" asked Rollison, for Jolly would have reached the extension by now.

"At m-m-my flat."

"And where is that?"

"Why, Chelsea. N-n-number 3, Globe Crescent."

Globe Crescent, Rollison knew, as did anyone familiar with south-west London and the arty set, the pop set, the dope set, the trend set and the dollies and the love people, was a lovely crescent of Georgian houses, four or five storeys high, the fronts overlooking the River Thames, Battersea Pleasure Gardens and its trees and lights. By some freak of anticipation by the architect, a contemporary of Mr. Nash, it had no view of the Battersea Power Station. According to the news on B.B.C.-2 a few hours ago, the Thames was likely to freeze over if the weather from the north pole did not change direction soon. Only a few days ago he had visited an old friend in Globe Crescent, and there had been talk of skating on the river. All of these things, of course, went through his mind in a flash, and for once he spoke again without prompting from the girl.

"And what is the trouble?" he enquired.

She seemed to catch her breath but there was no way of telling whether it was in fear or vexation. A brief pause heralded her answer:

"I'm—so frightened."

He could ask: "Of what?" He could assume that this girl—if in fact she was a girl and not an old lady with a deceptive treble—was on the lunatic fringe. But by now he was wide awake, and Globe Crescent was no more than ten minutes' drive from here at a time of night when the streets were clear. So he pushed back the bedclothes and began to get out of bed, saying:

"What floor?"

"*Four!* Y-y-you'll come?"

"I'll come," he promised, hoping he was not too much of a fool.

"B-b-b-bless you!" she cried. "Do hurry. P-p-please hurry!"

She rang off simultaneously with Rollison, and soon the door opened wider to admit Jolly, simultaneously with Rollison shedding his sky-blue pyjama jacket. Jolly began to open his mouth but Rollison answered the question before it was uttered.

"Yes, I *am* sure, Jolly."

"I was afraid you would be," said Jolly, still more despairing but, being wide awake, not looking anything like so ancient. "Will you need me?"

"Only to stand by in case of trouble," Rollison said. "Although I don't see good reason to suspect any at the moment."

"Don't you, sir?" asked Jolly, in a sepulchral tone.

"Do you?" countered Rollison, slipping into an undervest.

Jolly did not answer at once, but his expression answered for him. He did expect, or at least half-expect, trouble. It was not really surprising, reflected Rollison, as he put on the garments which Jolly handed him, including a thick woollen sweater of a dark green colour. In the thirty years during which they had been master and man, trouble had showered upon them; it had come from many unexpected quarters and been started by the most innocent and honest-seeming people; it had come from millionaires and paupers, from vagabonds and villains, innocents and fools. In fact, for very long periods it had never stopped coming at all. Some, especially newspapermen with a nice eye for a story, claimed that there was a magnetic attraction, in Rollison, for crime and criminals. Certainly over the years he had won a remarkable reputation as a private investigator, and of recent years had become so respectable that the police occasionally praised and almost invariably tolerated his activities. It was remarkable how many men (and women) had been imprisoned because of Rollison's activities; and many still languished behind the grey walls and the iron bars of such establishments as Dartmoor and Pentonville, Strangeways and Wormwood Scrubs.

It was quite possible, Rollison knew, that the stammering girl who had not given her name might be a decoy, to draw him out of his home for some nefarious purpose. It was equally possible that she was really in trouble.

He drew on the thick, ribbed sweater, and Jolly took a short but very warm and stylish top-coat from a wardrobe. It was camel-hair in colour, with dark buttons.

"What I don't understand, sir," said Jolly, "is why the young woman didn't turn to the police."

"Perhaps the police are not romantic enough for her," remarked Rollison.

He smiled, and his eyes sparkled. He cut quite a figure and looked deceptively young, as well as lean and lithe and powerful. He took a swagger cane from his wardrobe, and also a gold cigarette case, making sure that it was full. As he tucked it into his top-coat pocket, Jolly said with obvious relief :

"I'm very glad you're taking precautions, sir."

"As I grow older, I grow wiser," Rollison murmured. "If only a little. Well, I'm ready."

He strode out of the room, and to the lounge hall and the front door, taking a quick look at a spot above the lintel. There was a small mirror, in fact a cunningly concealed periscope, placed there to make sure that he and Jolly could see who was outside, if unexpected callers came; and to check whether landing and staircase were clear, if he was going out at a time of half-anticipated danger.

They were clear.

He opened the door—and the telephone bell rang.

He stopped, automatically, and looked round. There was an extension close to the door and Jolly was already stretching out his hand for it. Rollison closed the door softly, as Jolly said in his most impressive voice :

"This is the Honourable Richard Rollison's residence."

He held the telephone to his ear and turned a puzzled face to Rollison, then went on : "I will see, Miss. One moment, if you please." He placed his hand over the receiver, looked almost imploringly at the Toff, and said : "It is a young lady, sir, asking for you."

"Does she stammer?" asked the Toff.

"She hasn't done so yet, sir."

"Does she say what she wants?"

"Only that it is a matter of great urgency," stated Jolly.

Rollison held out his hand for the instrument, feeling very puzzled indeed.

The earlier call had seemed unlikely and this one seemed absurd; would two young women call him in the small hours of the same morning by sheer coincidence? He took the receiver and schooled himself to say in an aloof voice :

"This is Richard Rollison."

"Toff!" breathed a woman who sounded young and had a voice remarkably like the other girl's. "Thank gosh you're in !" *Gosh* again; but no sign of a stammer. Rollison felt as if his head was going round and round. *"Have you heard from Mary?"*

"And who is Mary?" asked Rollison, no longer aloof but truly baffled.

"Oh. You know. *Mary.*"

"I know some Marys, but . . ."

"Oh, please don't prevaricate," cried the stammer-free girl, and she was not simply pleading, she was commanding. "Have you heard from Mary?"

"Mary who?" demanded Rollison firmly again.

"My sister, of course ! Oh, *please* . . ."

"Young woman," interrupted Rollison, only partly pretending a note of exasperation, "I don't propose to allow you, your sister or any Mary to call me up in the middle of the night and then be rude. Now: what is your name?"

There was a gasp; and silence.

It would not have surprised him had she hung up, but there was no sound of that; in fact there was a hint of heavy breathing; as a girl in distress might breathe if she were suddenly confronted with a problem which had come right out of the blue. He waited. Jolly rubbed his lined forehead, and then suddenly turned and went off—presumably and belatedly to listen-in on another extension.

The girl spoke at last.

"Marie McGee," she told him, pronouncing the name Ma-*ree*.

"I'm afraid I don't know a Marie McGee," replied Rollison, very gently.

"Oh!" she cried. "But you must!"

"I'm truly sorry, but I don't," Rollison assured her. "But I can tell you this. A young woman who might be your sister Mary telephoned me about fifteen minutes ago. She asked me to go and help her in some acute problem which she didn't explain."

"That will have been her!" cried this girl. There was a pause again, which sounded very abrupt, before she went on : "Do you mean she didn't mention me?"

"She didn't mention anyone," replied Rollison. "And I don't even know who you are, except as the sister of Mary McGee."

"I'm Mar*ie*, I've told you," the girl said impatiently. "You mean—but you *must* know her!"

"I don't know her from Ad—Eve," declared Rollison.

"Oh, *gosh!*" exclaimed Marie. "It can't have been all fabricated, she—where did she ask you to go?"

Rollison very nearly told her, but before the words 'Three, Globe Crescent' fell from his lips he realised that this might be a very clever ruse to make him say where the first girl was. This caller might be Marie, sister of Mary McGee, and might be as ingenuous as she sounded, but there was no certainty. So Rollison said:

"Don't you know where your sister lives?"

"Oh, I know where she lives but I don't know where she is. Toff, she—*does* she call you Toff?"

"Only on the one occasion that she's ever spoken to me and if in fact it was your sister Mary, yes, she called me Toff. Why are you so worried?"

"She's in such danger!"

"Of what?" demanded Rollison.

"I can't tell you over the telephone. I—*Toff!* Please come and see me. I'm sure I could make you understand if we were face to face, but the telephone is so impersonal And I'm not far away from you, really. I'm in Knightsbridge, Number 11, Elm Avenue. Oh, please—"

"I will come and see you," promised Rollison, "just as soon as I can."

And he rang off.

He stood by the telephone for a few moments, staring at the periscope mirror, and was there when Jolly reappeared, thumbing the pages of the London Telephone Directory, L to R section. He placed it on a small table and Rollison joined him. He traced a finger down the Mc columns, soon pausing at the McGees. There were about forty or fifty but none was shown here as being at Number 11, Elm Avenue, Knightsbridge, or Number 3, Globe Crescent, Chelsea.

"It is very peculiar that neither is mentioned, sir," Jolly remarked. "You will be *very* careful, won't you?"

Rollison replied: "Yes, Jolly. Now let me see whether I can get away before the telephone rings again." He moved towards the door, adding under his breath: "What would make parents christen one daughter Mary and the other Marie?" He went out, with a smile at Jolly, half-expecting the telephone to start before the door closed:

but it did not. He looked back from the first landing, to see the door closing. He went down three double flights of stone stairs which were covered with thick haircord carpet, and at last into the street.

The cold struck at him, knife-like : he actually took in a hiss of breath.

There wasn't any wind, just the cold. It closed about him. It seemed to rise from the frosted steps and pavement and from the walls and dead, dark windows. It must have fallen ten degrees in the past few hours. The street-lamps had a halo about them, and frost was heavy on the fluted iron posts. A pale moon spread a strange light which dimmed the stars. He quickened his pace towards the corner of Gresham Terrace away from Piccadilly; just round the corner was a mews where he garaged his latest Bentley and a black Morris 1100, 'Jolly's' car. He turned the corner and a figure loomed over him and his heart leapt.

" 'Evening, sir," a policeman said.

"I—oh. Yes. Good evening. You scared the wits out of me."

"Just going about my lawful occasions, sir," the policeman remarked. A strong smell of tobacco wafted on his breath; he had been standing here having a secret 'drag'. "Where are you going, if I may ask?"

"To get my car."

"You live—oh! It's Mr. Rollison." The other's tone and manner changed, suspicion vanishing. "Didn't recognise you, sir, not at first I didn't. I wear contact lenses and on these nights they can get a bit misty, you know. You're out late, aren't you?"

"I'm answering an S.O.S. from a sick friend," Rollison told him, and wondered whether he was being too glib. But the other appeared to notice no such thing, and moved off, while Rollison stepped along the cobbled mews to his garage, opened the old-fashioned doors, not altered since this had housed a coach and four. The little car sat snug and demure, and its engine started at once. As he drove out the windscreen misted over momentarily, but soon cleared.

He chose the Grosvenor Place, Buckingham Palace Gate and Victoria way to Chelsea. The night was so still; the moonlight almost unearthly; the quiet, unreal. Every street-lamp, old-fashioned gas or flourescent strip, had a halo about it, the roads and pavements were white-rimmed. A car spun round the corner from Ebury Street, right across his bows. He braked and swerved, the other car swerved, tyres squealing, wobbled, straightened, and tore on.

". . . fool," Rollison growled.

Soon, he was on the Embankment, where the river reflected the moon and added a kind of iridescence. The tall houses, the squat modern blocks, the bridges, all seemed to be remote, almost in a different world.

Then, he saw the trees and the gardens in front of Globe Crescent. A few lights were on at the windows and every street-lamp was bright; so were the lights of a car double parked outside what looked like Number 3. He turned into the Crescent off the Embankment, intending to drive past, and perhaps to find room to park for his little car. As he passed, however, the front door of the house opened, and he saw an almost unbelievable sight.

A man came hurrying, with a girl over his shoulder!

At least, if the wildly kicking legs were any guide, his burden was a girl. Her head and shoulders were swathed in a blanket or a rug, and her arms were pinioned, too. There was no sound except the man's footsteps and, suddenly, the creak of an opening door. The double-parked car's engine roared as its nearside door swung open, the hurrying man seemed to hurl his burden into the rear seats, and then scrambled in. Before the door closed, a woman at the wheel sent the car shooting forward into the cold, cold night. Rollison recognised a Ford Cortina.

CHAPTER II

Chase

The car passed Rollison in his Morris 1100 as it slowed
down.

He did not turn his head but swivelled his eyes towards
it. The man was leaning over the back seat, as if to tuck
the girl's legs out of sight, the woman stared straight ahead
and gripped the wheel tightly, in the manner of a nervous
or inexperienced driver. Rollison, already moving, simply
drove a little faster, but caught up with the other car at
the turn onto the Embankment. The high street-lights
showed that the Cortina was red. The man was kneeling on
the back seat; it was impossible to tell what he was doing
to the girl, whose legs were out of sight.

Lights turned green; belatedly the driver put on her
flicker, and turned right, away from the heart of the city.
Rollison turned after them. A big truck, sides glistening
silver, bore down on them, and Rollison allowed it to pass
him. They were approaching Battersea Bridge, and he
would see if the car he was after turned either right or
left.

It went straight on.

The truck swung out, the woman driver was pushed
almost to the kerb. Rollison, behind the truck, followed
it closely. The woman driver, who looked to be in the
middle forties, still strained at the wheel. The man was
now sitting upright in his seat, facing front. He struck a
match or lighter as Rollison passed, to light a cigarette.

It showed a long nose and jutting eyebrows; quite a remarkable profile. Now Rollison in turn passed the truck, but before the turn-off just short of Lots Road Power Station, pulled into the side. Three more cars, all larger than the Cortina, passed at speed; then the abductor car came, and Rollison pulled out to follow. Nothing suggested that the occupants had noticed him.

"Which suggests they don't make a habit of this," Rollison said *sotto voce*, "or they'd be on the lookout. I wonder where they're going."

He soon discovered.

They went past the triangle of Eelbrook Common, dark in the centre but tree and lamp-post fringed, and took a turning to the left, along some streets of tall, Victorian houses. He saw them take a sharp left, and as he drove past the end of the street they turned down, saw their brake lights go on. He made a U-turn and when he got back to the street saw the Cortina at the side of the road. Both doors were open and the man was leaning inside from the pavement.

They were outside a small block of contemporary-looking flats which stood back from the level of the houses. No one was about. Rollison switched off his lights and pulled into the kerb, in time to see the man lift the girl out of the car while the woman looked up and down the street in a fury of anxiety.

The girl, carried now in the man's arms, was no longer kicking. Those slim legs that had been in such a frenzy, now hung limp.

Had he drugged her?

Or—strangled her?

He carried her into the driveway of the flats to the entrance, which was on one side, and the woman followed, hugging herself against the cold. As soon as she had disappeared by the side of the block, Rollison drove much closer, got out, closed the car door very carefully, and crossed the road. The cold struck him again, like a brittle curtain of ice.

No one was in sight, but there were shadows on the ground outside the entrance; moving shadows. He drew close to the front door, and heard a whining sound, peered round cautiously and saw the doors of a lift closing.

He stepped towards the front doorway.

There was a small rectangular foyer. On two sides were passages leading to flats whose numbers showed above the passage entrance; on one side, facing the front door, two lifts. Rollison strode through welcome warmth over a russet-coloured carpet and pressed for the elevator.

Its doors opened at once.

The panel on the side showed that there were five floors, and he pressed the button marked 5, the highest floor. It started up at once, very slowly. He felt impatient and really apprehensive for the first time. If the man had killed the girl—

Nonsense!

If the other had set out to kill, he would have slain her at Globe Crescent; the very fact that he had kidnapped her surely proved he wanted her alive. There could be some very simple explanation. If the girl—he had taken it for granted that it was Mary McGee—were in her early twenties as she had sounded on that telephone, the woman driver was old enough to be her mother. This could be a family fracas, dreadful for those involved but certainly no concern of the Toff.

The lift stopped and he got out.

There was no sign of anyone up in the passage here, and he stepped back before the doors closed and went down one flight. This time the doors opened onto a sharp click! of sound—the closing of a door. He stepped out. The doors of the lift by the side of his were closing, so he had the right floor. But the passage and the blank doorways leading off were all dark green anonymity, and he had no idea whether the couple had turned right or left. He turned left and strode along the passage. Four doors led off it, opposite the lifts, and on the wall running along-side the lift was another; there were five flats here, then, in all.

He saw light beneath one door, marked 4C, stepped to it, and pushed the small letter-box open; almost instantly he heard footsteps and a man speaking.

"How—how is she?" he asked, and Rollison was vividly reminded of Mary, stammering.

"She's all right," a woman replied.

"Sure?"

"Stop worrying, for goodness sake!"

"What a hell of a thing to say," retorted the man. "How can I stop worrying?"

"How much good will it do you?"

The man grunted, and heavy footsteps suggested that he had stalked away. A door closed. Rollison lowered the letter-box with great care, so that it made hardly a sound. Then stood up and examined the look of the door. It was a Yale type, which could be the most difficult to force and yet could be the easiest, if it had not been double-turned on the other side. The traditional way to force it open was with a piece of stiff celluloid or plastic which would 'creep' round the lock itself and, when it was exactly in the middle, would force the lock back.

He took out the gold cigarette case, shifted three cigarettes, and picked at what seemed to be the lining but was in fact a piece of strong but flexible plastic. He put the case away, then bent down to the letter-box. The man was speaking again.

"Do you want anything to eat?"

"No. Do you?" the woman countered.

"I couldn't eat a thing if you paid me," said the man. "My God, I'm tired!"

"Then go to bed," said the woman. Out of the car she was much more confident and unquestionably the stronger of the two.

"Sure she's all right?" the man demanded.

The woman said: "Safe as a hundred thousand pounds!"

She laughed; and, a few seconds later, the man also burst out laughing.

Now there was no need to wonder about motive. This was a kidnapping for ransom, obviously. But a hundred thousand pounds? Who was Mary McGee that the kidnappers could expect to get so much for her?

He drew back from the door as a clock from a neighbouring flat began to strike. One—two—three—four. He hadn't been out much more than half-an-hour! He shivered suddenly, warm though it was in here, and walked towards a radiator at one end of the passage. The metal was toast hot. He sat gingerly on the projecting ledge, and pondered.

The man and the woman had kidnapped the girl with conspicuous success. Certainly no one else had followed them, and there was no reason to suspect that anyone else had been aware of trouble, except possibly Mary McGee. No, Marie McGee. Mary was presumably the one who had been kidnapped. What should he do now? A call to the police would bring this to a dramatic conclusion, but the fact was he wanted to learn much more about it.

He shifted himself away from the ledge, which, incredibly, became too hot.

Suddenly, he stood up and began to smile; and the smile grew into a grin; and the grin became almost fatuous until at last he actually chuckled. He moved towards the door of Flat 4C, and this time saw a light go out. He waited for fully five minutes and then looked in again.

The flat was in darkness.

He walked away and peered out of a small window at the head of the stairs. The street looked so pallid and cold, and the moonlight glistened on tiles which were like silver. No one and nothing stirred. He returned to Flat 4C, and checked again, then began to slide the plastic into the lock. It made no sound. He worked very slowly

and precisely, and hummed *The Impossible Dream* song
from *Man of La Mancha* under his breath. Soon, he felt
the lock begin to move, and suddenly there was a sharp
click! and the tongue went back.

He felt his heart jump; and its beating was the only
sound as he stood and listened lest the click had disturbed
anyone in the flat or near-by.

No sound came.

He pushed open the door and stepped inside.

This was a narrow passage, with doors to the right and
left and a wide area beyond with other doors leading off;
there were seven in all. Only two were open—doors
opposite each other in the passage. He stood between them.
Rhythmic breathing, near-snoring, came from the right; it
was the man. There was a pale light in the room, and he
peered round the door and saw twin beds with a small
table between. For one startled moment he thought that
the woman was awake and staring; but it was a trick of
light and eye-shadow which hadn't been cleaned off.

He drew back into the passage, then put his hand inside
the room at keyhole level. His spirits rose as he touched
a key. He withdrew it slowly and, smiling very broadly,
closed the door with hardly a sound, then locked it from
the outside. The click of the lock was very faint but he
paused in case it had been heard.

There was only silence.

He stepped to the other open door, where there was a
double bed with a girl on it, her face lift softly by the
moonlight from the wide window.

She was—*lovely*.

So fair; so pale; so soft and gentle-featured.

A sheet was drawn up to her chin, so that only her face
showed. He could not recall having seen a prettier picture
for a long time, but he did not allow that to slow him
down. He went across and drew the sheet back, and what
he saw then he did not like at all. She wore a shift-type
dress, without sleeves, but a rope was drawn tightly about

her waist and tied, at both ends, to the iron frame of the bed itself, so that when she awoke she would hardly be able to move.

But she lay still; so still that there was little likelihood of her moving for a long time.

She hardly seemed to be breathing.

He saw that she was, however; there was the slightest rise and fall of her breast, a barely perceptible movement at her lips.

He took out a penknife with a blade he always kept razor sharp, and with great care cut the rope. It fell from her waist. Then he slid his arms beneath her and the blanket on which she lay, and lifted her bodily.

She was hardly any weight at all.

He turned towards the passage, the apartment door, the lift, pulling the apartment door behind him with his foot as gently as he could. There was a risk that someone would come up in the other car, which had disappeared from here; there was always risk, but the odds against meeting anyone at half-past four in the morning were very slim indeed.

In the lift, which travelled as slowly downwards as it had up, he looked down on the girl he took to be Miss Mary McGee. The concealed lighting in the lift was very good, and it showed her flaxen hair, her flaxen, upswept lashes, the peach-bloom delicacy of her complexion. Her hair was like spun gold, a little wispy at the temples and the ears. He guessed her to be twenty-two or three. The tiniest of lines were showing at her forehead and the corners of her eyes.

The lift stopped, the doors opened.

He had been so preoccupied in studying the girl that he had forgotten to be ready in case someone was in the foyer, and alarm surged through him. But there was only the sharp cold. He stepped out, into the ice-box of the night, and there was no one. He snatched a glance at the doorway and read : *Giss Street Apartments,* then actually reached the gateway to the street itself, before he heard footsteps. Swiftly, he drew back, and the cold clutched him as it must clutch at the girl. He held her more tightly, as if she were a child in swaddling clothes.

The footsteps were quite unmistakable.

A policeman?

No. There was a big man on the other side of the road, carrying a heavy parcel. Goodness knew how far he had carried it, but judging from his deliberate pace, for some time. He seemed to take an age and the cold was beginning to make Rollison's teeth chatter.

Suddenly, the man turned into a house opposite the Toff. He rested the parcel on the floor of the porch; fumbled for keys, and soon opened the door and disappeared. The sound of the door closing was quite loud.

No one else appeared.

Rollison took the girl to the car and sat her comfortably in the seat next to the wheel, went round and tucked the blanket and quilt about her. God! It was cold; now he began to shiver uncontrollably. But the engine wasn't affected, and soon he drove off in triumph. If anyone saw him now they would think he had a girl in the car the worse for drink. He laughed aloud, in deep delight, and said in a carrying voice:

"The kidnapper kidded! How's that?"

Then he said, reprovingly: "Don't be childish, Richard. You've work to do."

As he slowed down to take the corner he saw that he was in Giss Street, S.W.6.—in Fulham, in fact. He took note of the near-by houses and a small row of shops before heading for the West End.

Soon he reached Gresham Terrace, finding a place to park right outside the front door. He opened the door with his key, went back for the girl, rushed her into the house and closed this door with his foot. A hydraulic stop prevented it from slamming. He hoisted the girl on his shoulder and went gaily up the stairs, reached his landing

—and saw the door open. Jolly had been on the watch then. Blessed Jolly.

It *was* Jolly, who gaped at the burden in his arms, and then said in an auguished whisper:

"The girl Marie is here, sir. She says her sister has been kidnapped. Do you wish me to—"

Before he could finish, a girl out of sight called clearly: "Is that the Toff? *Is it?*" And she came, running.

CHAPTER III

Quick's the Action

Rollison had never needed to act faster in his life.

He could hear the girl, could not fail to understand her eagerness and sense of urgency. He spun round on his toes, dumped the unconscious victim into the corner, straightened up again and was facing the door with one foot forward when the other girl appeared, almost thrusting Jolly aside.

Then, Rollison had one of his greatest shocks; perhaps the greatest ever.

The girl who appeared in front of him was the girl he had dumped on the floor!

That was nonsense. Utter nonsense. It couldn't be true. But—

There she was. Tall and slender and wearing a blue and white striped dress, with flaxen hair wispy at temples and forehead. The only difference was that the sweeping lashes were over wide-open, eager, sky-blue eyes; and that she was moving. In fact she moved so fast that she almost fell into Rollison's arms but drew back with remarkable suppleness.

"Have you found her?" she cried.

"Found who?" asked Rollison.

"Oh, *please* don't prevaricate! Have you found my sister?"

"Jolly," said Rollison firmly, "I need coffee, sandwiches, my warmest dressing-gown and five minutes peace and quiet." He turned and looked severely at the girl. "If you are Marie McGee, I will see you in five minutes."

"But I've been waiting for hours to see you!"

"I haven't been out much more than an hour," Rollison retorted. "Jolly, take Miss McGee into the study."

"But—" the lovely blonde began.

"If you don't do what I ask I won't talk to you at all!" rapped Rollison.

Marie was so taken aback that she faltered, and then allowed Jolly to lead her out of this L-shaped lounge hall. The base of the L led to the study-cum-drawing room, the other to the domestic quarters. As soon as she disappeared, Rollison ducked out, picked up her unconscious double and carried her swiftly—into the kitchen, out through another door to a passage off which led his own and a spare bedroom. He dumped the girl unceremoniously onto the double bed and then went out and locked the door. As he turned round, Jolly appeared from the big room.

Rollison gave a thumbs-up sign.

"I'm very glad to know it," said Jolly with feeling. "Shall I tell you—"

"Tell us both together," Rollison said. "I'm serious about that coffee. The temperature must be nearly zero outside." He went into his own bedroom, opposite the spare room, stripped off his outer clothes and donned a camel-hair dressing-gown and some fur-lined slippers. Only then did he sit back in an easy chair to relax and recover. It was not the first time he had seen two people uncannily alike but he had never been more startled at first glimpse. He needed the few minutes to regain his breath and his poise, but he did not want to keep the other girl waiting for too long. If he judged her aright she was very near despair.

He got up and went out, hearing Jolly still in the kitchen.

He half-expected to see Marie McGee standing and

glowering or sitting and sulking. Instead, she was standing in front of his trophy wall and studying it openmouthed. She was so absorbed that she did not notice that the Toff had arrived, and she drew nearer the wall and stretched out her hand towards an ugly-looking knife with a chip in the blade.

"Naughty," murmured Rollison. "Don't touch."

She dropped her hand as if stung, and spun round.

"Oh, you scared me!"

"I'm sorry. I thought you heard me coming."

"No, I—" She narrowed her eyes but that did not take away their brightness, and her mouth opened in a little 'O'. "You *are* the Toff, aren't you?"

"It's a name some imaginative people gave me years ago in the East End of London," he admitted.

"You don't look at all—" She broke off and coloured faintly, so doing the impossible by looking even more lovely.

"At all what?" he asked.

"It doesn't matter."

"I'd like to be judge of that."

"Oh, all right," she conceded. "You don't look at all romantic."

"Oh, dear," sighed the Toff. "Nor glamorous?"

"No." She frowned at him and then said slowly: "You're teasing."

"Only a little," said Rollison demurely.

"*Are* these your trophies?"

"It's a word we use, although some may call them souvenirs."

"And *does* each one represent an arrest or something?"

Soberly, Rollison answered: "An arrest or a death, yes. How do you come to know so much, Marie?"

Marie McGee replied with great intensity: "Mary told me." And as the words came, tears sprang to her eyes, her slim body went rigid, her hands clenched. She tried to speak but her lips quivered so much that words would not come. She looked distraught, and she pulled at Rollison's heartstrings, although there remained a slight reservation in his mind : that she could possibly be acting.

Then Jolly came in, carrying a laden tray.

"I meant to tell you earlier, sir," he said in a tone which brooked no interference, "that Miss McGee finally went to her sister's apartment in Globe Crescent, and discovered the flat deserted and some indications of a struggle. She immediately came here to ask for your help. She - ah - was so distressed that I felt constrained to tell her that you had gone to Chelsea to see Miss Mary McGee, and that it was possible you had some idea where she had gone. Coffee, sir? Or tea?"

"Is it late for coffee or early for tea?" Rollison temporised, and then decided : "Tea. Marie, why on earth should your sister be kidnapped?"

The girl stared, as if blankly, and then answered mechanically : "For ransom, of course."

"Isn't that a remarkable thing to take for granted?" Rollison asked.

"I would have thought it the most obvious thing in the world," declared Marie, with a touch of exasperation.

"Why? Are you wealthy?"

"Gosh!" exclaimed Marie. "Where have you been hiding yourself? Of course my parents are wealthy. *McGee,*" she breathed, and so widened her mouth that for a moment she actually spoiled her beauty. "M-c-G-e-e-. *McGee.*"

Then Rollison realised who these McGees were; he should have realised it earlier, but the soup McGees were so much part of an enormous publicity build-up that they were more like characters in a comic strip than real people.

They had performed a kind of miracle, starting from poverty until today they almost rivalled Messrs. Heinz. From countless tins in countless supermarkets and grocery stores, on shelves, in cafés and canteens, comic-strip draw-ings of Mr. and Mrs. McGee looked down from pale blue labels. They were presented as parents, as head of a family who knew what was good for everyone, particularly in the evening. McGees' soups gave warmth, strength, security, vitamins, proteins, fats and every conceivable kind of goodness. There was no doubt at all that the McGees were worth millions of pounds, and that even a hundred thousand would be a comparatively small price to pay for the safety of one of their daughters.

Unaware that the penny had dropped, Marie turned almost angrily to the Toff, demanding:

"*Now* do you know who we are?"

"Yes," Rollison admitted. "The truth has dawned."

"Then *now* will you start justifying your reputation. Good gosh!" exclaimed Marie. "How on earth have you managed to acquire all those trophies if you aren't brighter than this? *Did* he win them all?" She spun round on Jolly demanding an answer imperiously.

"Every single one, Miss," Jolly assured her, and then astonished the Toff by adding: "I am sure that Mr. Rollison will make some allowances for your youth and for your obvious distress but there is a limit even to his tolerance. I most strongly advise you not to try it too much."

Marie McGee looked first startled, then abashed and next, quite suddenly, angelic. She smiled, and her teeth showed unbelievably bright. Her eyes became dewy; her body relaxed. She moved—it was almost a sway—towards Rollison, and held out her arms, so that quite automatically he enfolded her in his. She looked up at him with such appeal as she was cradled against him.

"Oh, Toff," she breathed. "Dear Toff. I'm so sorry— I really am."

He did not think for a moment that she was sorry; only that she wanted her own way and had come swiftly to believe that this was the best way to get it. Whom had she victimised before, to learn both trick and habit? Her father? A brother? Even an uncle or a friend? Not, surely, a lover. She looked so virginal. It was this thought which woke him to an awareness that he was softening towards her; she was so limp and warm and cuddlesome; kittenish.

He gave her a little squeeze, then put her firmly away from him, and for safety's sake poured out two cups of tea. Handing her one, he asked :

"Why do you think your sister was kidnapped?"

"Because she was threatened," Marie said.

"And you thought it was a serious threat?"

"Oh, yes," stated Marie, obviously resigned to the fact that there would be no immediate capitulation by this man. In the calmest of voices, she went on to make the most astounding of statements. "Somehow you get to know. People have always threatened to kidnap us. Daddy's so wealthy, you see, and so fond of us, proud is the word, I think, that he would do and pay anything to make sure we came to no harm. Ever since we were babes-in-arms we've been kidnapped or threatened with kidnapping. As a matter of fact, the threats seldom come to anything, and some are hoaxes, but now and again one does get serious, and somehow we always know. It's in the tone of voice when the kidnapper telephones, a kind of understatement you might say. It sends shivers through us, I can tell you."

She paused, and stared, not at Rollison, but blankly at the trophy wall. It was some seconds before Rollison could stop studying her and marvelling at her, so as to bring himself to say :

"And tonight it is serious?"

"Yes."

"Was the demand from a man or a woman?"

"A woman."

"Did she put a price on your sister's head?"

"She said she wanted a hundred thousand pounds," asserted Marie quietly, almost casually. She picked up a wafer-thin sandwich from which either minced ham or minced salmon oozed, and began to eat, daintily.

"Just like that," Rollison inquired.

"Oh, there was the usual blackmail threat," Marie replied, continuing to nibble.

"*Blackmail*? Not ransom?"

"Yes," answered Marie. "I suppose the truth is that even you are not as sophisticated and experienced as Daddy, Toff, and you don't know much about my family, do you?"

"Practically nothing," Rollison admitted, faintly.

"If only Mary were here, I'm so worried about her." There was a long silence before Marie went on: "Oh, I suppose I needn't be, yet, the next thing we'll hear is how to pay the ransom, and I suppose dear old Daddy will find a way to pay up." She went on, picking up another sandwich and looking very candidly at Rollison, "I don't really know whether he's a very wise man or simply addlepated. He's the sweetest, most angelic thing that ever happened, but—" She broke off again, as if appalled, and her voice rose: "Toff! Do you think I'm being too cynical?"

"Or detached," retorted Rollison.

"I suppose I must sound both. But we've had such an unusual upbringing and he's taught us certain standards which lots of people think are shocking, and we don't always seem to live in this world. We're in it but not of it," she explained: and took another sandwich.

"Marie McGee," Rollison asked, out of the blue. "How old are you?"

Without the slightest hesitation she answered: "Twenty-two. Why? What difference does my age make?"

"For twenty-two, you *are* either too naïve or too prac-tised in making fools of men," Rollison stated.

"And of course, you disapprove." She stood back from him, put her head on one side, and went on in a rather puzzled voice: "You are very old-fashioned, aren't you?

Quite the anachronism! And yet—" Her gaze wandered towards the trophy wall. "And yet you've done all that."

"Marie McGee," said Rollison, moving to the wall. He picked up a silk stocking lying on a small bracket and let it run across the palm of his hand. "A girl as pretty as you was strangled with this, because she thought she was so modern and with-it, whereas I was so old-fashioned." He saw a shocked expression leap into Marie's eyes, and held the stocking towards her but she did not take it. "This," he went on, replacing the stocking, lifting a small glass cover and taking out a lipstick in a golden case, "had cyanide of potassium crystals injected into it, and two girls of about your age were so cynical about old-fashioned anachronisms that they used the lipstick and were dead within twenty seconds. Cyanide both burns and suffocates. Wouldn't you rather be alive and ana-chronistic than with-it and dead?"

She stared as if with horrid fascination at the lipstick.

"The reason I'm alive and the reason that Jolly is alive is that although we often take very great risks—"

"Excuse me, sir," interrupted Jolly; and for him to stop Rollison in full flow was a rare thing indeed.

"Well?" Rollison was almost sharp.

"I think Miss McGee should be made to understand, sir, that you have never taken risks for personal gain or aggrandisement. Mr. Rollison's activities are always altruistic, Miss, and in the interests of other people who —like you and your sister—have come to appeal for his help."

"Ah," said Rollison, more gently. "Bless you, Jolly."

Marie now looked from him to Jolly and back and raised her hands a few inches, then dropped them to her sides.

"There are fifty-three trophies on that wall," Jolly went on, "and each is a memento of a crime or series of crimes with which Mr. Rollison risked his life to solve. Do you see the top hat?" It was atop the whole collection, a black and silky-looking topper with two holes in the crown. "The holes are bullet-holes, and large ones at that. And that small dagger? I drew it out of Mr. Rollison's back, terribly afraid that it had killed him."

Jolly stopped: and Marie held out her hands towards Rollison without any apparent coyness and with no cuddly sex appeal.

He took them and squeezed, not too tightly.

"Fashions change. Habits, manners, words and phrases, all of these change, but people remain pretty well the same, Marie. And one unchanging characteristic of the young is that they think their elders square. As often as not they're right in some ways but they make some ludicrous mistakes." He squeezed again, let her go, and sat on the arm of a large leather-covered chair. "Why did Mary turn to me? What made her so frightened, and what has frightened you? When I know the truth I may be able to help, but I really must know the whole truth."

"Yes," agreed Marie, huskily and with her cheeks flushed and her eyes suspiciously bright. "I know that now. I'm sorry if I—well, I'm sorry." She drew a deep breath. "Well, we had this threat. At least, Mary did. A woman said she wanted a hundred thousand pounds or she would be killed. Instead of telling Daddy as we always do, she kept it to herself. She said she was tired to death of having him buy her safety. She wanted to see it through herself. Then—well, then she got scared, but it was too late; Daddy flew to New York yesterday. We didn't know what to do, until Mary decided to appeal to you. Someone's told her an awful lot about you, and she passed on most of it to me on the telephone tonight. She felt absolutely positive you would help, and I can see now she was right. It didn't occur to her that you would be too late."

"Well, she left it pretty late herself," Rollison said, drily.

"Yes, I know, she—well, apparently she just got scared

out of her wits tonight. She was hoping to stay with friends in Globe Crescent, but they were away. She used their apartment, we all have a key to it, but—well, she's disappeared. I telephoned there but didn't get an answer, so I dashed over to see and then came rushing round here when I saw she'd gone. You will look for her, won't you?" When Rollison did not answer, and was in fact deliberating whether to tell her that her sister was only a room away, a different, harder expression came into her eyes, and a harder note into her voice. "It would be worth a great deal, Mr. Rollison. If you find her *I* would guarantee to pay you at least fifty thousand pounds. And I *can* afford it. I shall get two million pounds from a trust my father settled years ago on my twenty-third birthday, only six months away."

It was Rollison's turn to harden, and Jolly's to cover his eyes with his hands.

"Will you help?" Marie almost screamed. *"Or do you want even more?"*

CHAPTER IV

Spoiled Brats?

For a moment or two Rollison was almost angry at the idea that he could be bought, but anger was a worthless thing in itself and there was no point in venting it on her. So he pursed his lips and shook his head, and said in the silkiest of voices :

"I do not help spoiled brats, however charming and pretty or wealthy." He put a hand up when she began to speak, and the gesture made her stop so that he could add : "How did Miss McGee get here, Jolly?"

"In an open sports car, sir, parked across the road. I happened to see her arrive."

In fact, he had been watching; it was his way to be wary.

"I will go and get her sister, who has had an injection of morphine, if her pinpoint pupils don't lie," Rollison said. "I'll carry her down to the car."

"You mean you *found* her?" gasped Marie McGee.

"I mean that I wasn't as late as you thought," said Rollison coldly. "See Miss McGee to the landing, Jolly." And he stalked out of the room.

A moment later he saw Mary, the twin, lying so still— and he actually pulled up short, the likeness was so striking. But he did not hesitate for long. He bundled her up in an eiderdown and hoisted her to his chest. The door was wide open and Jolly and the girl had disappeared; he fancied he could hear their footsteps on the stairs. As he turned the bottom landing cold air swept up, as if from arctic wastes. A moment later he heard the front door slam. Turning the landing he saw Jolly behind the door, obviously waiting to open it. His teeth were chattering.

"She is g-g-going to put the hood up and the heater on," he stammered. "I should w-w-wait a moment, sir."

"Let me out now and you hurry upstairs. I don't want you ill," ordered Rollison. "This girl's as warm as toast, and it won't take Marie long to get home."

Jolly opened the door, obediently.

As Rollison stepped out, wind struck at him; and it seemed savagely colder. His clothes might have been made of paper, they were so thin, absolutely no protection at all. Marie already had the engine on and the car hood half up; welcome heat was blowing in, and he lost any compunction he had felt. He placed Mary in the seat next to the driving wheel and, without a word, helped to secure the hood. The metal angle joints snapped into place, and for a moment he and the girl stared at each other over the roof of the car. It might be the peculiar shade of the street lamps, but Marie seemed blue with cold.

"I suppose it's no use saying I'm sorry," she said.

"You need to learn what Mary learned—trying to buy what one wants isn't always the best way to get it," Rollison said sententiously. "Get in before you freeze to death. Where will you go?"

She didn't answer but ducked into the driving seat. The door slammed and the engine roared. By the time he was across the street, the M.G. was snorting towards Piccadilly. Whether she went to Globe Crescent or Elm Avenue, she would be at her destination in ten minutes. He wondered whether either place had a lift, then told himself that it would do Marie McGee no harm to exert herself. He opened the door, and as he stepped into the

comparative warmth of the hall passage, was seized by a
fit of shivering. He ran up the stairs, and the fit had
passed by the time he reached the top. There, the door
was on the latch, not fastened, and he went in and
closed it. Jolly appeared from the big room, where
obviously he had been tidying.

"Jolly," Rollison said.

"Yes, sir."

"Was I right to be so harsh on a night like this?"

"Indubitably," answered Jolly, without the slightest
hesitation. "You caused her no actual hardship, and the
young woman has had her own way far too long."

"Yes," Rollison said. "A truly spoiled brat."

"In the sense that she expects any male to bend to her
will under the seduction of sex-kittenism or money," Jolly
said. "Whether this will do her any real good it is hard
to say," he went on, almost primly, "but she will certainly
have no further illusions about you, sir." There was a
momentary pause before Jolly added with surprising
vehemence : "The impudent young hussy !"

"Yes, indeed," said Rollison. "Jolly."

"Sir?"

"I know you must be tired out. Don't set your alarm
clock for the morning, we can both do with a couple of
hours sleep-in before we start making enquiries. But
before you go back to bed, tell me something."

"If I can, sir," murmured Jolly.

"*Why* did Marie McGee come?"

"I beg your pardon, sir?"

"Did she simply want help for her sister?"

"I certainly got that impression."

"Yes. But the whole affairs smacks of the improbable.
A call at three a.m. Another soon afterwards. Did they
really denote an emergency, or was there any degree of
ruse about it?" When Jolly didn't answer but looked
shocked, he went on : "I saw the sister being carried off,
I think I saw a man actually drugging her in the back

of a car; certainly she was unconscious when he pulled her out. I followed him and a woman to their apartment in Giss Street, Fulham, and when they were asleep took her away. Her pulse was a little slow and her eyes pinpoints—she'll be conscious in a few hours."

"You actually kidnapped her from her kidnappers!"

"That's what I thought. But it's all a little too coincidental and peculiar. Almost as if everything had been carefully planned in detail to inveigle me into the affairs of McGee. Even," Rollison went on, "to the wilful attempt to exasperate me and to make both you and I deliver a little homily."

"I don't quite see why they should carry out such an elaborate hoax," Jolly protested.

"Hoax," echoed Rollison. "Just the word. I do. Jolly."

"Yes, sir?"

"I think the McGee sisters are in some kind of trouble and want my help for some very different reason, but don't want me to know what that reason is," stated Rollison.

Jolly studied him for a long, a very long time. Then he shrugged his shoulders slightly, and remarked: "It is conceivable, sir. I—ah—I really think we should go to bed. It is after half-past five."

"Ah," said Rollison, aloud. "Bed." And under his breath, he added: "You think I'm crazy, don't you, Jolly? We shall see."

It was good to get back to bed.

He expected to find his mind so full that sleep would come with difficulty but in fact it came almost at once. His last waking thought was not of Mary or Marie McGee, but of the icy blast when the front door had opened. Tomorrow was going to be by far the coldest day of the winter, but he would have much to do. In the centrally heated comfort of his bedroom he curled himself up and went to sleep, vaguely aware of the sound of traffic, of the morning, for by then it was after six o'clock. He slept on, oblivious of milkman, policeman, newspaper boy and early-about pedestrians; oblivious of the increasing cold, the howling wind, the gradual dawn, the schoolchildren in their waistcoats, bright red and yellow so as to defeat the danger of cars driven by men and women only half-awake.

It was half-past ten when he woke. There was no sound in the flat, but Jolly would keep particularly quiet when he was sleeping. He yawned. It was chilly. He sat up. It was quite cold, in spite of the central heating. His mouth was dry. He got up, put on a dressing-gown and looked out of the window, onto the unprepossessing cement and concrete and iron fire-escapes at the back of these old buildings; a mews which had been bombed during the war, and all picturesqueness had been blasted away. A butcher, carrying a tray, moved with jerky steps, as if trying to fight the cold. Rollison went into his bathroom, which led off the bedroom, rinsed his face and went into the passage.

There was no sound or sign of Jolly.

He went next to the kitchen, a room which Jolly kept immaculate. A small window was ajar in the larder, which was as cold as any refrigerator. He had never known it so cold in the flat. He touched the radiators and found them hot; at least they were trying. He made tea, and took it into the big room, placing it on the large, pedestal-type desk in front of the trophy wall. The silk stocking, the dagger and the top hat all reminded him of Marie McGee.

What had really been in her mind?

Was she simply spoiled by too much money? Or had there been an ulterior purpose in her visit? There was no grounds for thinking so, yet he could not get the possibility out of his head; he did not think he really knew the purpose of her visit. He went to the front door and took the newspapers out of the wire letter-basket beneath the letter-box itself. The headlines were about strikes and rumours of strikes, wars and rumours of wars, and an escape to West Germany from Czechoslovakia. What a world to live in! He yawned, sipping the welcome hot tea, spread a newspaper over the desk and stood, drinking and reading. On a morning when he had felt less like pampering himself he might not have read so thoroughly; as it was, a tiny paragraph on an inside page gossip column caught his eye.

> Playboy millionaire Rupert McGee missed his flight to New York yesterday, after being stopped by the police while driving along the M4 motorway at over a hundred miles an hour. Mr. McGee did not lose his temper, but his daughter, Marie, who was driving him, gave the police a piece of her mind. Some say she slapped the policeman who stopped her papa, who caught a TWA 747 instead of his scheduled BOAC.

It was a silly little paragraph, in its way, and he would have been far less intrigued had it not been for Marie and Mary, and the fact that Marie had told him that her father had left for New York. She had driven off last night as if she were quite capable of driving at a hundred miles an hour along Piccadilly.

"So Papa McGee *is* in New York," Rollison mused, and finished the tea. He left the newspaper open on the desk, adding: "I wonder if I ought to call Jolly," and went towards Jolly's room.

It was after eleven o'clock, Jolly would probably be annoyed with himself for having slept so long. He might forgive himself for not getting breakfast, but if he missed preparing lunch he would feel it was a catastrophe. His room was off the passage which led to the kitchen, and it communicated with a bathroom and the approach to the spare bedroom. The door was closed. Rollison, unused to calling his man, tapped first lightly, then more loudly; there was no reply. He opened the door cautiously, and the first thing to surprise him was the ceiling light, full on. The curtains were drawn, too, and Jolly was a fresh-air and broad daylight fiend.

Perhaps the bitter cold had made him change his ways.

Then Rollison looked round the door, to the bed; and realised that Jolly wasn't there.

He stared stupidly at the rumpled pillow and the turned-down bedclothes. Jolly had been to bed, of course he had, before the telephone. The state of the bedclothes was evidence of nothing. The light—the drawn curtains —well, Jolly had got up in the middle of the night, he might have drawn the curtains to make sure he wasn't visible from the windows opposite.

The bathroom?

"Jolly!" called Rollison.

There was no reply.

He did not really understand why he was suddenly filled with fears; but he was. His heart beat fast and his breathing was shallow. He went to the bathroom, calling Jolly's name. In an alcove on the right was a bench and some shelves, where Jolly stored his photographic equipment and the paraphernalia he needed for his criminological studies. For Jolly took crime and his employer's reputation very seriously. He had all facilities here for taking finger-prints; he had a microscope, a ballistics projector for showing two slides at once and matching markings on bullets, a shelf full of chemicals with which he could test for bloodstains and in fact most ordinary stains. He liked to be able to give Rollison near-professional help, and in some cases, he did.

The bathroom door was closed.

"Jolly!" cried Rollison, and turned the handle and pushed.

The door opened onto an empty bath and empty bath-room.

"Where the devil is he?" Rollison asked aloud.

He strode back into Jolly's room, into the kitchen and the spare room, every corner of the flat, but he found no sign at all of his man. His heart thumped much more loudly than ever. Had Jolly gone out shopping, he would have left a note; whatever he had gone out for he would have left word, unless he wanted to keep it secret.

Why should he want to go out on a secret errand?

"Clothes!" cried Rollison, and almost ran back to the bedroom.

There were Jolly's clothes on a clothes stand beside the wardrobe; striped grey trousers, lightweight black jacket, and pearl-grey cravat. On the tray were loose change, wallet, keys, a handkerchief, a penknife and a book of matches. Shoes and socks were by the foot of the clothes stand, the shoes brightly polished. Jolly had placed everything ready for the morning, but had not dressed.

Rollison opened the wardrobe. There were other suits and some hanging shirts and even a sports jacket and flannel trousers; and there was a raincoat and a light-weight overcoat. But a heavy blue Melton which Jolly had had for ages wasn't there.

Had Jolly taken a suit and the overcoat and just walked out?

"Nonsense!" Rollison exclaimed aloud. "He simply couldn't do it!"

That was the moment when he saw the smear of lip-stick on the pillow : on *Jolly's* pillow.

He stood and stared, even more disbelieving than before. Jolly did not take young women to bed with him. Jolly did not take *women* to bed—certainly not here; Jolly's personal, family and even emotional life were things apart from his life at the flat, and Rollison had occasionally wondered over the years whether the elderly relatives he always claimed to be visiting were in fact relatives; even whether he had a love-life. Certainly that had never been discussed.

It *was* lipstick.

It was pale, pale pink lipstick.

It was the colour of the lipstick which Marie McGee had worn. Rollison could imagine it now, as she stared at him, her lips parted, the lipstick looking almost transparent.

He bent down and touched it with his little finger. It smeared, and a smear came off.

Oh, this was crazy! Jolly, missing : Jolly, with lipstick on his pillow, lipstick which could be Marie McGee's. Jolly—

The telephone bell went, startling him, for the bell was loud and clear. He picked up the extension on Jolly's bedside table, and discovered that he was breathing too hard to speak clearly, so he drew a deep breath, to help steady himself, while he heard a girl with a familiar sounding voice and a hint of exasperation, calling :

"Are you there? Are you there?"

At last Rollison had his breath steady enough to state simply : "This is Richard Rollison."

"Why on earth didn't you answer?" demanded the girl whom he felt quite sure was Marie McGee. "Mr. Rollison, I must see you urgently. My name is Maria McGee."

CHAPTER V

Mary, Marie and Maria

Rollison was silent for perhaps ten seconds. Thoughts warned him that this young woman might at any moment reproach him again for not answering. He himself felt waves of disbelief assault him fast on the waves of bewilderment over Jolly. He thought he heard an intake of breath at the other end of the line, herald of an outburst of impatience, and forestalled her by asking:

"You do mean Maria, don't you?"

"Of course I mean Maria."

"Not Mary or Marie but Maria."

"Yes!" she cried, and made the line quite quiver. "The McGee triplets, is that enough for you?"

"The McGee triplets?" he enquired, much more mildly than he felt.

"Of course! Who else—"

"You couldn't be one of—" Rollison hesitated, heard the girl's shallow breathing, and then without quite knowing why he gave a little laugh and finished : ". . . one of the trip-trip-triplets?"

There was a pause. It lengthened. And then came another searing intake of breath and the girl who called herself Maria McGee exploded:

"This is not funny!"

"Mary, Marie and Maria McGee have certain humours of their own," Rollison said. "One of your parents must be a great jester."

"You leave my parents out of this!" Maria cried.

Rollison had seldom been nearer to putting down the receiver without saying another word. He had had far too much of the triplets McGee. Two of them behaved as if they needed their bottoms spanked, talking with an imperiousness which only years of utter spoiling could cause. "Toff do this, Toff do that." "I must this, I must that."

Two things persuaded him to deal with Maria cautiously: the fact that Jolly was missing, and the fact that lipstick which looked very like Marie's was on Jolly's pillow. He needed information, not antagonism.

"Why do you want to see me?" he asked mildly.

"It's confidential, and—"

"Before I even consider seeing you, I want to know what it's about," Rollison interrupted, much more sharply.

"I tell you it's confidential. I won't talk about it over the telephone. If you know what's good for you you'll come at once."

Very slowly and deliberately, Rollison replaced the receiver. If he allowed himself to be hectored and threatened by any or all of the sisters McGee he would know no peace of mind at all. Already he felt sure he would need all possible peace of mind before this strange affair was over. He looked down at the pale pink lipstick again, frowned, gave a funny little grin, and went out and into his bedroom, then into his own bathroom. This was no time to bath: that telephone would ring again in a minute or two. He was not a devotee of the electric razor but they had their moments, and this was one of them. He washed and shaved quickly, dressed as quickly. Ten minutes or so had passed since he had hung up on the girl; she had been longer calling back than he had expected. The little minx—if minx was the word!—knew how to play on nerves. If he were any judge, two out of three triplets McGee were experts in manipulating men. He, the most hardened, sophisticated and least impressionable of men, was already beginning to feel uneasy. Of course, he wouldn't be but for Jolly.

The telephone bell rang.

"There she is," said Rollison confidently.

He must not look as if he had been waiting on the call, so he turned slowly to his bedside telephone, and paused before lifting the receiver. Simultaneously there was a ring at the front door, always disconcerting when the telephone bell seemed at its loudest.

"This is Richard Rollison," he said. "Will you please—"

"*Is my sister there?*" a girl cried.

She sounded like Maria but she could be Marie—and for all he knew, Mary might now be awake and, when awake, might speak like either or both of her sisters. But what about her stammer?

"Hold on and I'll find out," he said. He heard protestations squawking from the receiver as he strode along the domestic passage towards the front door. It might not be one of the McGee girls. It might be anyone—even Jolly! He glanced up at the periscope mirror over the lintel, that security device which had saved him so much trouble over the years: and a girl stood there, visible in miniature through the glass.

She could be Mary; or Marie; or Maria, as far as he knew.

It was ridiculous! It was preposterous. It was true.

He opened the door.

This girl, suddenly life-size, was quite beautiful. Her hair was blonde and fell about her shoulders, her eyes were cornflower blue, her complexion quite unbelievably perfect and her lipstick, not overdone, was exactly the same colour as that on Jolly's pillow.

She did the last thing he expected: stood back a pace and stared at him as if she were astonished.

"Good morning," he said. "Which triplet are you?"

"Why," she breathed, "you're so *young.*"

This little devil was flattering him now! All the sisters

seemed to have acquired the arts of seduction and married them to arrogance; were there such things as identical triplets?

"Yes, and sometimes I feel even younger than I look," he said.

He did not quite know what possessed him, but as he stretched out his hand with over-elaborate greeting, the impulse to draw her close and then heave her onto his shoulder, was overwhelming. So he took her hand; and before she could have the faintest idea of what he intended, her wrist; then, with a quick twist of his body he placed a hand on her hip and lifted her. He spun round, as she settled, lightly, on his shoulder, pushed the door to with his elbow, and carried her into the big room. There, he lifted the receiver, and said very precisely:

"Yes. Your sister is here."

He lowered the triplet to the desk and sat her on it gently.

Now, he was a man; a human male; and he could not fail to be aware of the suppleness of her body, the yielding of her bosom as she slid from the desk. He was, moreover, a greatly experienced man in affairs of the heart; and indeed with women, from the virginally innocent to the coquettish, the promiscuous and the—for the sake of nicer word—courtesan. And as he felt her body he knew that she deliberately pressed against him; deliberately made him aware of her as a woman. And she must have decided to do that as she came out of her semi-shock from being lifted high.

She turned the incredible beauty of her eyes towards him as she spoke into the telephone.

"Hallo, darling," she said. "Here I am." There was a brief pause before she leaned back, and her mini-skirt was not made for leaning back when her waist was on eye-level to an impressionable man. It would not have been so bad had she crossed her legs. Instead, she giggled. "No, darling," she said. "I think he's delicious . . . Have you

seen him? . . . Well, perhaps you weren't seeing at your
best! . . . Really? . . . Yes, I'll tell him . . . How is Mary
. . . Thank goodness for that! . . . Oh, I really don't think
he will give us very much trouble . . . I'll be back by one
o'clock for certain."

Slowly, she rang off.

Slowly, she slid off the desk.

Slowly, she approached Rollison until they were only
inches apart. She looked into his face, moving her head
with slow deliberation. My goodness, those eyes! Tilted
backwards, her head was only on a level with his chin. She
smiled. She didn't move and didn't seem to breathe: just
smiled. And in her face and eyes and by some strange trick
also in her body, she was seduction itself.

"You won't give me much trouble," she said. "Will
you?"

And, still moving slowly, she slid her arms over his
shoulders and round his neck.

He did not know what warned him, but the warning
came, in a blaze of red. He felt her fingers cold on his
skin, wriggling, as if to interlock; and he saw an expression
in her eyes, a new glint of sharpness, of anticipation. Then
he knew what she was really up to. She would lock her
soft hands round his neck and have him in an unbreakable
hold : one which could actually break his neck, or be used
to throw him over her shoulder or right or left or wherever
she wanted him to go.

Vixen was the word.

He ducked.

The disappointment on her face was quite ludicrous.
She grabbed, which was a mistake; she should have danced
back out of his reach. Without effort he placed his hands
on her waist and hoisted her high and when she kicked
at his face he simply twisted so that she was upside down.
She wore pantie-hose and beneath them panties of darker
hue. He twisted again, so that she went round three or
four times in a kind of whirling wheel. When he stopped,

holding her upright in front of him, she was too dazed
or breathless to kick. He carried her to the largest armchair in the room, a comfortable Regency one covered
in bottle-green velvet, and placed her in it with exaggerated gentleness.

Her hair was dishevelled, her lipstick smudged, her
colour was higher, her skirt rucked up higher still, she
was taking in short, sharp breaths so that her mouth was
open all the time and he could see her teeth. It was not
fair: nature had been too kind to her, no woman with all
her other attributes *should* have teeth like pearls.

But hers were.

She looked even more beautiful than she had at her cool
and calm and composed best.

He smiled at her, unaware that there was a glow in his
eyes and a red tinge in his cheeks, which added to his rare
good looks; and his hair, a little ruffled, gave him a slightly
raffish look.

"Would you like some coffee?" he asked.

She drew a deeper breath, and said: "You must be the
most handsome man I have ever seen."

"You must have been locked up in a nunnery," he
retorted.

She drew her brows together momentarily puzzled; and
then burst out laughing. It was a deep, pleasing, happy
sound. When it died away she relaxed more in the chair,
and nodded.

"Yes, please—I would love some coffee."

"I won't be two jiffs," he said.

In fact the percolater was primed in the kitchen. He
plugged it in and went back to the passage to see what
this McGee girl was up to. In the most natural way
possible she was sitting back in the chair and appeared to
be studying her face in the mirror set in the lid of a small,
square, white handbag; she had a comb in her right hand.
He went back and returned in five minutes with plain
biscuits and chocolate biscuits and a big percolator still

bubbling and spurting out wisps of steam. She was now standing in front of the desk and studying the trophy wall; tidy again, she looked unbelievably like her sisters. The tiny waist, the slightly flared skirt with a hemline only just below the curve of the bottom, were as eye-catching as any he had ever seen. So were her legs.

As he placed the tray on a table by the big chair, she spoke without turning round.

"*Are* these all yours?"

"I think you ought to ask your sister."

"No. Seriously. *Are* they?"

"Yes."

"*Is* each one a lethal weapon?"

"Yes."

Now she turned and looked at him with those enormous eyes, and slid almost in a whisper: "One which might have killed you?"

"A lot of them were used with that intent."

"But I don't understand," she remarked, as if bewildered.

"How can you when you've only just seen the trophies?" asked Rollison lightly. He moved across to pour out coffee. "White or black?"

"White, please—and it's not that I've only just seen, I've heard about the trophies. Mary's made a deep study of them from newspaper articles, and—well, you don't look old enough!"

"Really?" But this time he did not think that this was simply flattery, nor even flattery with a purpose.

"To have done all this, I mean."

"I'm quite old enough."

"And to be so—famous."

"Maria," Rollison said firmly, "Stop being naïve and come and have some coffee." He pushed a smaller chair into position for her and sat back in his own. "What is all this about constantly being under threat of kidnapping?" She didn't answer. "Did Mary say whether she had any

idea who her abductors were last night?" There was still
no answer but Maria picked up her coffee and a chocolate
biscuit, then began to wander about the room, examining
the trophies and then examining him.

Her wilful silence angered him, but he kept his temper
under control. Sooner or later he would make her answer,
but this wasn't the best time.

He ate some plain biscuits and drank coffee, trying to
guess why she had come and what the sisters really wanted
of him. A curious fact was that he felt quite calm and at
ease with her: not angered, not even troubled or even
exasperated, although with anyone else he would have
been seething with impatience.

As curious was the fact that she showed not the slightest
umbrage at the way he had handled her; in fact that
manhandling might never have happened. At last she stood
firmly in front of him, legs close together: delicious.

"So Mary was right," she remarked.

"In wanting me to help her?"

"In wanting you to help *us*."

"All three of you?" asked Rollison, startled.

"If one of us is in trouble, all three of us are," explained
Maria.

"Oh. The identical triplets," he suggested. "I had
wondered."

"In a way, yes," said Maria. "And this time—well, I
think we really are in need of help. I expect Marie told
you that Daddy was away. And you know that Mary was
actually kidnapped—how *did* you get her back?"

"I have my methods, Watson," Rollison replied
earnestly. "How is she?"

"Sleepy, that's all—too sleepy to be mad. Apparently
the kidnappers were waiting for her when she left the flat,
and she didn't have a chance." She paused, looking at
Rollison thoughtfully, before adding: "How did you get
her?" When he didn't answer, she went on: "I suppose
it's no use asking you to divulge too much. Well, the im-

portant thing is that you can work a kind of miracle."
She finished her coffee, held out her cup, said: "I'd love
some more. May I?" She picked up another of the chocolate biscuits and went on speaking in exactly the same
tone of voice: "Will you help us, Toff? Please? We really
do need help."

"If I may say so, you've gone a funny way about
persuading me. My greatest temptation has been to spank
you all and send you packing." He handed her more coffee
and she took it, frowning, and then backed away a pace.

"Yes, I know. We're so used to getting our own way
that we get mad if we don't. Mary's by far the nicest one
of the three of us. Anyhow, that's beside the point. We
need help because we don't want to be kidnapped. You
see, whenever we are, Daddy pays, and he has enough
other troubles on his mind without that. We really want
protecting." She finished, and her blue eyes had never
seemed more candid or more appealing. "*Will* you protect
us?"

"Provided you release Jolly at once, I think I will," said
Rollison.

And although his tone was light and there was a smile
on his lips, his eyes were cold and demanding.

CHAPTER VI

Missing Jolly

It was difficult to be sure of the expression in Maria McGee's eyes. She was so skilful at covering up, could turn from sex kitten to cat and then into a nice, wholesome young woman and in a flash to one of remarkable naïvety. Perhaps, of course, she was all of these, possessing a kind of vari-split mind. More likely, she switched from pose to pose at will. But if he could judge her at all, he judged that she was genuinely surprised at his words.

"I don't understand you," she said, simply.

"It's very easy to understand. You or one of your beautiful sisters and possibly some boy-friends managed to get in and take Jolly away from this apartment during the night."

She frowned in apparent perplexity, and after a moment asked: "Why on earth should we?"

"To twist my arm."

"To twist your arm?" she echoed, as if wonderingly; then suddenly her face cleared, and she actually laughed. "You mean, you think we kidnapped your man so as to make you help us?"

"Yes."

"Dear Toff," she almost cooed. "You don't know us very well, do you? We have *much* more faith in ourselves than that, it wouldn't occur to us that we might need some form of coercion to win you over." Now, her eyes were dancing. "But what a lovely idea! I'm almost sorry we didn't do it."

"One or both of your sisters could have," Rollison declared.

"Oh, no," she replied, "we wouldn't make major decisions on our own. And until today it wouldn't have occurred to me that we might need outside help to persuade you."

"What made you change your mind?" demanded Rollison.

"Fishing?" she enquired.

"Fishing? I—oh." He laughed. "Yes! Do you mean my performance when you arrived made victory seem less certain?"

"Yes," she answered. "I've never met anyone quite like you." Her gaze wandered towards the trophy wall, then quickly back. "I suppose the truth is there *isn't* anybody. Toff—" She paused.

"Yes?" He was very wary of her change of tone and mood.

"We didn't take Jolly. What makes you think he's been kidnapped?"

This was a difficult question to answer. Nothing had been said or even hinted; it was simply his certainty that Jolly wouldn't have gone off without leaving a word if he had had any choice. There might be no positive evidence but there was what the police would call circumstantial or *prima facie* evidence, and he felt no shadow of doubt.

"Many indications," he said.

"Why?"

"I have no idea; that is, if you have told the truth."

"Oh, I have!"

"Then I've no idea at all."

"Was there"—her gaze faltered this time—"any other case going on?"

"None."

"Then it's either a new one coincidental with ours, or

else to do with ours."

"I am not a great believer in coincidences of that kind," Rollison remarked.

"No—nor am I. Toff, dear Toff." Again she paused and again he prompted.

"Yes?"

"I certainly did nothing to entice Jolly away. I don't believe my sisters did, either. I've heard quite a lot about Jolly. Mary—" Maria broke off, and shrugged, and turned and took another chocolate biscuit, biting it almost with savagery. "Mary first thought of asking you to help. She had a boy-friend once who worked on a London evening newspaper, the *Echo* I think it was, and he whetted her appetite about you, showed her a few articles and really built you up. But Marie and I were sceptical, if it hadn't become so urgent we wouldn't have agreed to ask you for a thing. The point is, no one knew we were planning to, so—" She broke off, looking very perplexed indeed, and then shot at him: "Do you see what I mean?"

"I think so," said Rollison.

"You have to do better than *think*," she flashed, and imperiousness showed for the first time for nearly an hour.

"Yes indeed. Reason," Rollison said. "You are suggesting that if Jolly wasn't kidnapped for some coincidental reason, then he must have been kidnapped to prevent me from helping you. As no one but the trip-trip-triplets knew anything about your appeal to me, how could anyone else have known I might help?"

She pondered that reply for what seemed a long time, and then she said in a wondering voice: "You know, you really are quite clever."

"How nice of you to say so," murmured Rollison.

"Oh, dear!" she exclaimed, contrite in a moment. "Did I sound terribly patronising?"

"Very patronising indeed."

"I'm afraid it's the age gap," she excused herself,

stretching out to touch his arm as if in solace or reassurance. Her fingers were so beautifully kept; and soft.
"You know there was a time when anyone over fifty
was trenchantly patronising to anyone under twenty-one,
and today there's a kind of swing of the pendulum. But it
doesn't affect the issue, does it. If no one knows we hoped
you would help us, no one would have any reason to try
to stop you by switching your attention to Jolly. So there
must be a coincidence."

"Or," said Rollison.

"Or what? *Please* don't be pompous!" How her eyes
could flash!

"Or one of you triplets"—he had the greatest difficulty
in preventing himself from stammering the word—"let
the cat out of the bag."

"It's utterly impossible!" she declared.

"Maria," said Rollison, "you would be surprised how
easy it is for cats to slip out of bags."

She stared at him as if he had mortally offended her,
and then she asked in an icy voice: "What on earth
made you imply that any of us had anything to do with
kidnapping your man? And isn't he old enough to look
after himself?" The second part of the question was
positively waspish.

"Come and see," he invited, and held out his hand.
For a moment he thought she was going to knock it
aside, but instead she took it and he led her past his
room and the spare room and into Jolly's. The light was
still on, but the blinds were drawn, and the general
appearance of the room was one of being over-lit. He
pointed to the lipstick, without a word. She glanced at
it, then turned to him and said witheringly:

"Jolly *is* a man, isn't he?"

"He is."

"And presumably, *not* senile. Or *is* he? Or are you
jealous of him, Toff? Do you keep him as a pet, and—"

Rollison had meant to keep so calm; yet make her

tell him all she knew. He needed to find out, for Jolly's sake. Instead, that was the moment when he lost his temper.

He must have signalled a warning with his eyes, for she dived towards the door, but he flung out an arm so that it was like a bar across her flat stomach, and she gasped and recoiled. Remembering how strong and skilful she was, he grabbed her round the waist and bent her over his knee, and thwacked her with the silver back of Jolly's hairbrush. Slender she might be, but she was solid, and the thwack, thwack, thwack sounded loudly and created some kind of echo, sounding almost like 'thwackity-thwack, thwackity-thwack'. At last the noise stopped, and he let her go. She backed against the bed, nearly fell, then moved towards the door. All colour save a spot on either cheek had gone, her pallor had a ghastliness and her eyes a glittering brilliance.

"For that," she said in a thin voice which seemed to crack with rage, "I ought to castrate you."

Then she strode imperiously from the room, into the big room, came back in a flash for her coat and handbag, then left the flat. He was only just in sight when she went out of the front door, and it slammed. He went slowly to the window and stood on one side, looking down into the street. A dozen people were in sight, including two nursemaids and the postman, but no one appeared to be watching this house—25 Gresham Terrace. His flat was designated 25G. He peered further to the right and left, and caught sight of a gleaming pale-blue M.G. sports car, which looked almost too new to be true. A moment later, Maria McGee swung into sight.

She stepped into the road, forcing the post van and a small car to swerve, but she did not glance at either, and neither driver honked in protest. But all the men in sight turned their heads and all but one of them stared. So did the two nursemaids. And Maria, that little skirt tight about her thighs, was really a sight to see. Even from this height, she seemed to wear nothing much beneath the skirt.

Ignoring everyone, she opened the offside door of the sky-blue beauty, forcing a cyclist to swing out; but all he did was to turn his head to watch a flurry of those long legs as she climbed in. Instantly, it seemed, the engine turned and the car roared forward. It swung out, missing a staid Rover in front by a coat of paint, and shot forward. He thought, but wasn't sure, that she glanced upwards when she passed Number 25, but she could not possibly have seen him.

The roar faded; the car disappeared.

The people in the street below were all smiling except an elderly woman who was staring in fright and disapproval. But despite her arrogant disregard of everyone else in the street, Maria had left behind her a trail of lifted hearts.

The Toff's was not lifted.

The Toff, turning back into the room, admitted the most unlikely thing to himself.

He was shocked. The young woman was so beautiful, but such talk smeared both youth and beauty. There was something else; she had sounded as if the threat was serious. Threat? It hadn't been phrased as a threat, yet the sound of her voice and the look in her eyes had made it one.

He was far from blameless, too; the disappearance of Jolly had got under his skin. There was something about the McGee sisters, too, which made him rise too quickly to anger.

Could he blame her for being so furious?

She must have been spoiled all her life. Her father must be unbelievably indulgent, and it was doubtful whether any form of correction had been administered for a long, long time. Yet she was in her early twenties; at an age where pride could be so easily hurt and dignity so easily affronted. And to be spanked—

Well, it was done now; and he began to think that perhaps good had come out of his angry beating. It had provoked a savage quality in her he would never have suspected. If that was true of her it might also be true of her sisters.

"Forewarned," he declared to the room, swinging round to the trophy wall, "is forearmed." He actually laughed at his own triteness, and moved towards his bedroom. What a morning. Jolly—

Jolly.

Maria had told him she knew nothing of Jolly's disappearance and that she was sure that her sisters knew nothing, either. The only trifle of a clue was the smear of lipstick on Jolly's pillow case. Maria had worn the same shade as Marie. He gave a little shiver. He turned into Jolly's room, but before he could do more than glance at the pillow, the telephone bell rang. It was the extension for the whole flat, not one which Jolly had for his own use, with an extension in the kitchen.

Could it *be* Jolly?

As he lifted the telephone, he felt a flash of wild hope; and his voice was very brisk as he said :

"This is Richard Rollison."

There were the squeaks telling of a prepayment box call : *peep-peep-peep-peep*. If Jolly were on foot, in need of help, even anxious to tell where he was he might nip into a telephone kiosk.

"*Peep-peep-peep—*"

"This is Richard Rollison," Rollison repeated.

The *peeping* stopped, a man spoke, and it was not Jolly. Rollison was so disappointed that his attention lapsed and he didn't catch the first words; but those which followed soon made sufficient impact. The voice was deep and pleasant and assured, and there was a slight, very slight, trace of accent. South African? Rhodesian?

". . . and I hope you won't need telling twice. Don't

help the McGee girls. They are poisonous little vixen and they could fool an impressionable man like you. Don't help them, Toff. Have I your word?"

The man broke off, leaving a taste of menace in Rollison's mind; and, because of the circumstances of this particular day, a touch of fear. Obviously the other expected him to speak, but he was breathing hard and did not want to betray any sign of anxiety. In any case, silence could puzzle the other man, and baffling the opposition was always a good thing. So the silence which he had begun in anxiety continued in deliberation; he naturally felt better, as if he were dictating terms at last.

The man spoke again, much more sharply.

"Are you there?"

"Oh, yes," said the Toff, quite nonchalantly. "I'm here."

"Then why didn't you answer?"

"I will answer when a question is worth answering."

It was the other's turn to pause; but this did not affect Rollison, who felt very much more in control of himself. The other was breathing shallowly, and, as the call was from a call-box, there would have to be a limit to these long and pregnant pauses.

"Rollison," the man stated flatly, "I am not fooling."

"Who are you?" asked Rollison, lightly.

"You'll find out soon enough. Have I your word that you won't help any of the McGee girls?"

It was rather funny; as if the man were putting him on his honour.

"No," Rollison answered, mildly.

"Don't play the fool!"

"I'm simply being honest," murmured Rollison, in the same mild manner. "Give me a good reason why I shouldn't help Mary, Marie and/or Maria if I feel so inclined."

The man said: "Don't fool."

"Don't stall," retorted Rollison.

"*I* stall!"

"What else are you doing?"

Again there was a pause, and at last Rollison felt a sense almost of triumph; that he had silenced the other. But the silence did not last for long and the triumph only a split-second longer.

"I shall tell you once more," the speaker said in a voice he no doubt meant to sound deadly. "If you help the McGee girls, I shall personally cut your man Jolly's throat."

The threat was like a slash from a knife: as bad and swift as the vicious way in which Maria had spoken. It not only drove away triumph, it brought back stark fear for Jolly. Yet as he realised what kind of threat this was, he realised another, vital fact. He could not give way to blackmail; he could not bow to threats, even though they were to Jolly. He never had, he never would. Jolly would be the first to agree, and yet—

The man at the other end of the telephone said: "I mean it, Toff," and rang off.

CHAPTER VII

Facts About Jolly

Very slowly, Rollison put down the receiver. As slowly he turned again towards the lipstick on the pillow, then deliberately away. It was almost incredible to imagine a girl's lips, a woman's lips, on Jolly's pillow case; to imagine a woman lying next to Jolly. Already, he had briefly considered the fact that Jolly's personal life, private life, call it what one would, belonged in a half-world away from this apartment. Now, he began to think more about Jolly, and this continued as he went into his own bedroom and, belatedly, began to dress.

He had known Jolly all of his life. His man, in his, Rollison's, boyhood had been first a footman, later a valet, at the Rollison family home in Norfolk, not far from the Broads. He could remember the stern-faced, dry-voiced man who seemed to be aloof from the rest of the staff, even to hate them, being discussed by his long dead mother and his father, alive today in his nineties and likely, it seemed, to live forever.

"The man," his beautiful mother had said, "is a misanthrope, Richard."

"The man," his tall and somewhat forbidding father had said, "appears to be able to handle the boy."

"But if he regards the rest of the world's people as a species to avoid, is he good for Richard?"

"Anyone who can handle that young man is good for him," his father had said, positively. "Don't separate them,

FACTS ABOUT JOLLY 63

my dear. Richard needs a mentor."

"But Jolly—" his mother had begun.

"Shall we review the subject a year from now?" Rollison's father had suggested, in a manner which meant: The subject is closed.

And so it had been.

So Rollison, when not away at school, had found himself guided and protected and even counselled more by Jolly than anyone else. Only he knew, although his father had obviously discerned, that whenever he was in need, Jolly was at hand. When poaching, or out in the small hours, when confronting human beasts who tortured and tormented animals, when running with his flailing arms into a crowd gathered about a secret, wholly unlawful cockfight, Jolly was there, to soothe by his very presence, sometimes to protect, sometimes to do battle alongside him. When in trouble with his father for such offences as climbing the church steeple and placing a pot on its weathervane, even when under threat of expulsion from school for refusing to name accomplices, or breaking the rules by forcing entry into a near-by girls' school, Jolly had been at hand.

There had come a time when he, Rollison, had wanted to find his own feet, and he had travelled the world, by cargo boat and tramp steamer, by train and bus and occasionally by an aeroplane which seemed fated to crash. He had lived alone for nearly two years. He had learned much. He had come upon much crime and some evil and most of the hard facts of life, and he had come to believe there was much good in people, if only they were left alone, and had enough to eat and drink and company when they needed it; and man or woman, abed, as their sex craved. He had learned a lesson begun at school, that there were pirates and parasites all over the world, preying on the poor and the ignorant and the meek. And he had come to hate crime with a ferocious bitterness which had sprung from his very nature.

Encouraged, as he now knew, by Jolly; not Jolly in the flesh and of the rather glum voice and manner, but Jolly out of the past, ten thousand miles away.

"If the odds are *too* heavy, Master Richard, either live to fight another day, or else outwit your enemies."

"You cannot defeat ten men at a time, but you can easily defeat ten men *one* at a time."

And once: "He most prevails who greatly dares," in a tone of great dignity.

In all these years, Jolly must have led a private life but it never obtruded on the youthful Rollison. When Rollison had returned, toughened beyond belief, handsome enough to make even sophisticated young women stare, bold and brave enough to take on not ten men but, for instance, a powerful London gang or the whole of Scotland Yard, he was told nothing of what Jolly had been doing. He had taken it for granted that Jolly would be free and willing to serve him, and Jolly had been.

They had moved to 25G, Gresham Terrace, over a quarter of a century ago.

Rollison, with much of this in his mind, said in a pained and muted voice: "Oh, my God."

For he had taken Jolly so much for granted, not meaning to, not even conscious of it. And he had believed the man when he had said he went to see relatives, and friends, on his days and evenings off. He had never heard a murmur of a girl or woman friend, had regarded Jolly as a kind of personal eunuch, less de-sexed perhaps than indifferent. Neuter-sexual. And yet there had never been such a man as Jolly, whose cold courage could sometimes put the Toff to shame, who spoke up without hesitation whenever there was need to disagree. He had always been available, seldom taking a holiday unless Rollison himself were away.

When he, Rollison, had been away, what kind of life had Jolly led?

Had he, Rollison made it virtually impossible for him

to lead a normal life?

At that stage in his reflections, many of them touched with pain, Rollison was fully dressed in a tweed suit of greenish-grey, a turtle-neck sweater to face the rigours of the day, brown shoes polished until one could see one's face in them—by Jolly, of course. Everything here was by Jolly.

Was that true?

"Much of it is," he said aloud. "Take Jolly away and this place would fall to pieces."

He relied on, leaned on Jolly, depended on Jolly, needed Jolly.

Whether or not the present crisis made him oversensitive on some of the sins of omission, whether he was conjuring up visions which had no basis in fact, whether Jolly was simply a natural man's man, truly eunuchal, one fact was absolute: Jolly had spent his life in serving him, Richard Rollison, who came not simply first to him but who had absolute priority.

And there was another absolute fact: whatever the cost, in money, time, effort and resources, he had to rescue Jolly. None of the ordinary rules served; if he had to break every rule in the book, he had to find Jolly.

Soon. But how?

What he mustn't do was take chances with Jolly's safety.

He stood in front of the trophy wall as he picked up the telephone. There, beneath the top hat with two bullet-holes in it, a hat Rollison had been wearing at the time of the shooting, was a furled umbrella. Jolly had once saved his life by using that umbrella as a spear; in nearly every case represented by a trophy, Jolly had played a part, often significant, sometimes vital.

Rollison telephoned a Whitechapel number, and soon a man with a Cockney voice answered against a noisy background of talk and laughter.

"Blue Dawg, Wapping. Whossat?"

"Richard Rollison. Is Bill there?"

"Bill's too busy to—" There was a curious gasp, a long pause, a louder, near-raucous background noise, before the Cockney asked in a breathless voice: "Who did you say you was?"

"Richard Rol—"

"The Toff?" Interrupting, the voice took on overtones of awe.

"The Toff," agreed Rollison obligingly.

"'Arf a minnit, Mr. R," the man pleaded. "I'll fetch Bill."

Someone laughed, on a high-pitched, near-drunken note, yet there was little drunkenness these days at noon, especially in an East End pub. The man yelled: "Bill! Someone important wants yer!" A gust of laughter followed, a muffled voice said : "Important? Didn't know Bill Ebbutt knew anyone important!"

Rollison could picture the scene so well. There was a telephone on the wall between the public bar and the saloon. The pub, old-fashioned and with sawdust on the floor, would be crowded with dockers, workers from a near-by canning factory which took meat straight from the holds of the refrigerator ships from Australia, New Zealand and the Argentine. There would be sailors and dock workers and a few policemen as well as a mixture of ex-boxers and chopping-block heavy and light weights who lived on Bill Ebbutt and his gymnasium, next door.

Suddenly, a man with a deep, wheezy voice growled: "Who's so bloody important?"

In the background there was a laugh from the man who had answered the telephone, and undoubtedly Bill Ebbutt suspected that he was having his leg pulled. But Rollison was in no mood for give and take conversation; and he said quite simply:

"Jolly."

Again there was a gasp; a deep, wheezing breath; and then Ebbutt said soberly: "So it's you, Mr. R. What's this about Jolly?"

"He's vanished," Rollison stated. "Kidnapped, I'm afraid."

"Good Gawd!" gasped the man whose name was Ebbutt; and after a pause he asked: "Since when?"

"Early this morning."

"Is it—is it *serious*, Mr. R?"

"I think it could be very serious," Rollison said. "As far as I know he was kidnapped so as to bring pressure on me."

"I can imagine how you go for *that*," breathed Ebbutt. "What can I do?"

"Send someone to the flat who can at least cook bacon and eggs, answer the telephone and take care of callers," Rollison said.

"Can do," promised Ebbutt. "Next?"

"How many men can you rustle up to stand by in case of need?" asked Rollison.

"For general work?" enquired Ebbutt.

"Yes. Legwork, probably tailing and bodyguarding but not necessarily me. Looking through a house or flat, scaring the wits out of a man—everything, Bill."

Again there was a pause. The background noises became more obtrusive, Ebbutt's breathing seemed to be through a sodden cloth. In his mind's eye Rollison was looking at a small election poster on the trophy wall, which exhorted: *Vote for the Toff*. In that investigation, Ebbutt had been injured and very nearly died.

"Give me an hour or two to sort that out," Ebbutt said at last. "I can fix it, all right, but we don't want any chances over Jolly—we want the best men we can get. Will you be at the flat indefinitely?"

"Until someone arrives to take messages," answered Rollison.

"Mr. R," said Ebbutt, in a tone of voice which warned Rollison that he was uncertain of the reception his next words would get, "must it be a man?"

"Who—oh. Jolly's locum?" Rollison was taken com-

pletely by surprise, for he had often used one of Ebbutt's
men at times when Jolly was overworked or off duty; and
occasionally, had used a man and his wife. Now, he went
on: "There could be some rough stuff, Bill. That's the
only reason a man might be better than a woman."

"Well, the flat would be watched, wouldn't it?"

"Yes. Who have you in mind?" asked Rollison.

"Well, if the Wrightsons' were at home I'd send them
but his ma's ill, dying of cancer they think, could be a
long job. And—" Ebbutt was beating about the bush, most
unusual for him, and suddenly spoke much more quickly.
"Do you remember young Toni Sapelli? Best young fly-
weight since Jimmy Wilde, that's my opinion." Vaguely,
Rollison did remember a dark-haired London-Italian
sparring in the ring at Ebbutt's gymnasium. "He got
knocked off the other day. Bloody crane driver dropped a
load of machine parts. 'Orrible. And he'd only been
married a couple of munce. His widow's looking for a
temporary job, needs something to occupy her mind, if
you know what I mean. Good cook, too—used to cook at
a canteen, and she's been doing the bar-cooking here but
she needs a place where she doesn't see Toni wherever she
looks, if you know what I mean. You'd be doing her a
favour, Mr. R."

"Send her," Rollison said, quietly.

"That's the ticket! Be there inside the hour—any ob-
jection to me bringing her over meself?"

"That would be a good idea," Rollison enthused.
"What's her name?"

He had a momentary thought that she might be Marie
or Maria, and almost held his breath. If she were, how
could he stand it? If—

"Rose," answered Ebbutt. "Rose Sapelli. Don't know
why but no one ever calls her Rosie. Okay, Mr. R. I'll
get started on the standby helpers and bring Rose over.
My Gawd," he went on, taking in one of his asthmatic
breaths, "I hope Jolly's okay, Mr. R."

He rang off.

Rollison's gaze shifted from the umbrella Jolly had once used as a weapon to the election poster, as he put down the receiver. This room was strangely silent, and the snort of a sports car which sounded right beneath the window was very loud; it also reminded him of Maria McGee. He held the telephone down for a few seconds and then lifted it, heard the dialling tone, and dialled a Mayfair number. He was answered immediately by a brisk-voiced woman.

"This is the Marigold Club. Can I help you?"

"Is my aunt in?" asked Rollison.

"Oh, Mr. Richard! Yes, I think so. Hold on, please."

His aunt was Lady (Gloria) Hirst, whom he had known since his irreverent youth as Old Glory. In that youth, even in the pre-Jolly days, she had often done battle for him, and she had meant much more to him than his mother. Because of this there was a bond between her and Jolly which was much tighter than most.

Soon, she said in her deep, authoritative voice: "Good afternoon, Richard. How are you?"

"Worried out of my skin," Rollison answered, and told her why quickly and in some detail. As he talked, thoughts flashed through his mind: that Old Glory owned and ran the 'Marigold Club' which was really a kind of hostel for young women in a variety of emergencies. Over the years it had salvaged the lives of hundreds of women hurt and bewildered and lost in the velvet savagery of the social world; and there was much goodness in her. At last, he finished, and he was thinking: If I had to hide any of those triplets away I'd choose the Marigold Club.

"Richard," his aunt said, "I will help in every way I possibly can. I will set aside everything I am doing, giving this absolute priority." There was a pause, before she went on huskily: "Is there anything I can do now?"

"One or more of the triplets might need temporary housing," Rollison said.

"You have only to let me know, Richard." The husky voice seemed to break as she went on: "Please don't delay a moment. You must find Jolly. Have you told Ebbutt?"

"Yes. He's getting ready to help."

"Excellent! And—"

Lady Hirst paused, and in the pause there seemed to be a moment of extrasensory perception; as if he could read her thoughts. What he read was something which had hovered on the edge of his consciousness but not demanded full attention. Now it did, even before his aunt said:

"Have you talked to Mr. Grice?"

"No," Rollison answered. "Not yet."

"Then you should, at once," Old Glory declared, the authority in her voice even more assertive. "This is not a matter in which you can neglect the help of Scotland Yard. Mr. Grice will be as concerned for Jolly as you and I. He will want to help. I hope you will get in touch with him immediately."

It was virtually a command.

Soon, thought Rollison.

"Soon," he said, very quietly and almost diffidently. "As soon as I'm sure it won't do more harm than good."

"Richard," said his aunt with great precision, "in this case you simply cannot afford to procrastinate. You must discuss Jolly's disappearance with the Superintendent. Quite apart from the fact that Jolly is in such urgent need, you have yourself to consider. If, through your failure to call on every possible source of help, Jolly were to come to harm, you could never forgive yourself. I *beg* you to telephone Mr. Grice at once."

CHAPTER VIII

Police—or No Police?

For Old Glory to say 'I beg you' was remarkable in itself; almost unique in Rollison's experience. Vividly, it reflected on her feeling and her fears for Jolly. Rollison did not feel that he could say: "All right, Aunt Gloria, I will," yet he wanted to give her some kind of reassurance.

"The moment I'm sure it won't do more harm than good, I will," he promised her.

"Richard," she said, forbiddingly.

"Yes, Old Glory," he said softly.

"Richard," she repeated, "I presume you have seen the obvious."

"I hope I've seen all there is to see," he hedged.

"I am beginning to doubt if you have. Whoever has done this thing must be aware of the great affection you have for Jolly. He must know how much it will hurt and affect you, might even put you off balance. Had you realised that?"

Rollison said, almost wonderingly: "Few people could even guess—"

"Don't be ridiculous," interrupted Old Glory sharply. "This man must be fully aware of your reputation, he would not expect to influence you by abducting a servant. He obviously realises that Jolly is like a member of the family. So this miscreant could well be someone with whom you have been in conflict before. Therefore you should consult Mr. Grice. He has records, you have only

recollection and Jolly is an absent *aide mémoire*. Richard,
I repeat—I *beg* you to consult Mr. Grice at once."

Almost grudgingly, Rollison conceded: "The moment
I'm sure it's the right thing to do."

"And please make sure I am told of whatever develops,"
his aunt said in a hard voice which faded into a long
pause; but soon she spoke more gently, more like the
woman he knew. "I'm terribly sorry about it, Richard. I
know how much it must hurt."

She rang off.

Was she right? Rollison wondered. Certainly he hadn't
taken it for granted that the kidnappers of Jolly knew the
kind of effect it might have on him. His first reaction had
been that Old Glory had seen an aspect, with her hawklike
mental vision, which he had missed, but was she right
about that, too? He was certainly aware that he must
consider it; the facts did not justify rushing to the police,
not even to his old friend Grice. True, Grice could find
out who lived at 4C, Giss Street Apartments, but so could
Ebbutt's men.

He could not do much until Ebbutt's Rose Sapelli had
come, he decided. He could not leave the flat without someone here to take messages, to answer if by chance Jolly
called.

He sat at his desk within inches of the telephone and
began to make notes so that he had a record of exactly
what had happened. He put in only approximate times
and all the details he could think of:

> 3.05 a.m. approx. Awakened by telephone. Mary
> McGee had pleaded with him to go to see her at
> 3 Globe Crescent, Chelsea.

> 3.15 approx. Marie McGee had telephoned and
> pleaded with him to go to her at 11 Elm Avenue,
> Knightsbridge.

3.30 approx. He had reached 3 Globe Crescent to see a girl being carried out; the girl had proved to be Mary.

3.35 approx. He had followed the man and woman kidnappers in their dark Cortina to a block of flats in Giss Street, Fulham, gone in and brought Mary away.

4.30 approx. He had returned with her to Gresham Terrace to be told by Jolly that *Marie* McGee was at the flat. Marie had been apparently desperate for him to go and rescue her sister. Marie had a lot of second-hand knowledge of him, and was fascinated by the trophy wall.

4.40 approx. He had discovered that the sisters were the 'soup' McGees, only rivalled by Heinz. She talked about frequent threats and apparently some kidnapping with father always coming to the rescue. She talked of 'usual blackmail threats' too. She wasn't sure whether her apparently beloved father was 'wise or addlepated'.

Rollison paused in his recollection, and then actually uttered the next words aloud as he wrote them down:

"We've had such an unusual upbringing and he's (Daddy) taught us standards which lots of people think are shocking."

Well, he *had* been shocked, later, by the sister Maria whom he had not known existed when Marie had passed on these confidences. A flash of doubt entered his mind. Were those confidences true? Or had she been making up a farrago of nonsense? After a pause he decided that everything had come from her lips too swiftly for there to be many lies. She had meant what she said in a desperate anxiety to win his interest and his help.

Then she had talked of being tired of relying on her father; of Mary's determination to help herself; of her confidence in the Toff . . .

"Well, she got scared, but it was too late. Daddy flew to New York yesterday."

Then, when he had stalled, Marie had shown a different, ugly side; next, had offered him fifty thousand pounds to find her sister Mary, declaring she would soon be wealthy in her own right; and when money had not impressed him she had almost screamed : *"Will you help? Or do you want even more?"*

A truly spoiled brat, he had called her; but how much less spoiled, in the event, than Maria!

5.30 or so. He and Jolly had gone to bed.

10.30 or so. He had woken, made his own tea, completely unaware of Jolly's disappearance, read about Marie giving the police a piece of her mind : oh, the *Globe* had called Rupert McGee the 'playboy millionaire' and that was somehow in keeping with Marie's talk of an unusual upbringing and being taught 'shocking' standards. 'Playboy' McGee—

10.45 a.m. He had discovered Jolly was missing, and seen the smear of lipstick.

10.55 or so. *Maria* McGee had telephoned, in her imperious way. Soon she had arrived and flattered him and he had treated her as a normal young woman until, once crossed, she had shown herself even more of a spoiled brat, a shrew far more vixenish than her sister Marie. But at least it had become apparent that although Mary had been the first one to suffer, all three sisters wanted his help.

What a peculiar way to go about getting it!

Then he had offered to help in return for Jolly's release —and had been assured that they knew nothing about Jolly! Mary, it seemed, had learned a lot about him, Rollison, from a boy-friend who worked at one of the London evening papers : the *Echo*. He would know of the importance of Jolly to the Toff. Sweet-tempered one moment, spiteful the next, she had made that crack about him and Jolly. He had spanked her and she had torn off in a rage, the pale-blue sports car had roared away. Before long . . . he jotted down another note:

> 11.45 or so : The unknown man had telephoned to say that he had Jolly and was holding him hostage, to prevent the Toff from helping the triplets McGee.

Now, the time was nearly half-past one. Less than twelve hours had passed since the abrupt waking. And what had he done? Practically nothing. Before he wasted time in self-reproach, he ran over what he had done and what his subconscious mind had planned, too. He knew as much as he could about the situation; had geared his friends to action; knew at least three places he could visit to find out more about the McGees. Once Rose Sapelli arrived he would be ready to go.

He went into the kitchen, prepared himself a biscuit-butter-cheese-and-bread lunch and had nearly finished when the front door bell rang. Ah: Rose! He went hurrying, and glanced up at the periscope mirror almost by force of habit. And then he stopped in his tracks, for his visitor wasn't a girl, it was a young man whom he had never seen before. Rollison studied him, as far as he could in the miniature reflection. He was dark-haired, rather lean, with thick, wavy hair. There was a hint of impatience about him; two or three times he glanced at his wrist-watch, and then he stretched out his hand, obviously to

ring again. The sound started and the door opened almost
at the same moment, and the young man, suddenly life-
size, darted back in surprise. His eyes were big, brown,
luminous, his complexion sallow and quite without blemish.

"Oh."

"Good morning."

"Mr.—Rollison?" The youth recovered.

"Yes," said Rollison, making no move.

"Mr.—Mr. Rollison," the young man said, "I—I'm
Adrian Bell." When Rollison showed no sign of recognition,
the young man went on : "Of the *Echo*." He gave a flash
of a smile as if he knew that now the *Echo* had been
mentioned there could be nothing but welcome. "Can you
spare me a few minutes?"

The Toff did not budge.

"What about?" he asked.

There was a pause; in it, this young man's appearance
and manner changed. He looked older and he looked
bolder. He straightened, and so looked taller. He smiled
with all the confidence in the world, and answered:

"Your manservant, Jolly, among other things. *Has* he
been kidnapped?"

After a very few seconds Rollison absorbed the shock.
He still did not answer, but his manner relaxed as he
spoke :

"Was it Mary, Marie or Maria who told you about that,
Mr. Bell?"

The open mouth and the gulp which ensued convinced
him that it had been one of the triplets. At last he stepped
aside, motioning Bell to come in. Bell recovered quickly,
and answered with a chuckle:

"Guess."

"Maria."

"Right in one."

"Are you known as Mary's boy-friend?"

"I'm a bit ubiquitous, really," stated Adrian Bell,
following Rollison into the big room. His gaze wandered

but his attention didn't. "I serve as escort to any one of the trio when they're in need. That is, when they don't want a boy-friend who will tell them how beautiful and seductive and bedworthy they are. I suppose I do spend most time with Mary, she—" He broke off, as if aware that he was talking too freely, and now took in the whole of the trophy wall at a sweeping glance. "She's been very interested in you, Mr. Rollison. May I offer a word of warning?"

He was such a boy.

"Please," said Rollison humbly.

"Don't believe a word any one of them says about motivation. They are all cannibalistic over men. They eat them. Old and young and middle-aged, they devour men as a regular diet. What did you do to make Maria hate you with such venom?" he added, innocently.

He had such guileless-looking eyes.

"I think you must ask her," retorted Rollison.

"Oh, I did, but she wouldn't say. So you must have thwarted her over some vital matter. Did she offer you her beautiful body, only to be spurned?" When Rollison did not answer but was in fact slightly shocked, Adrian Bell went on: "If you'd accepted she would have denied you, becoming virtuous in fact if promiscuous in fancy."

"Which is she really?" asked Rollison, now fascinated.

"Do you know," said Adrian Bell, "I honestly don't know. I've no personal experience with her. I've heard some men boast how rewarding she is and others ask if she's human. But—about Jolly. Has he really been kidnapped?"

"For the Press, I prefer to say he has been out on an errand and is later returning than I expected."

"You don't want publicity, in other words."

"Not yet."

"Anything you tell me is strictly off the record," Adrian Bell promised, quietly.

"Thank you. When I've a statement to make I'll see you

get it first."

"Thank *you*. Did you actually rescue Mary from kid-napping?"

"If I say yes and you print a story, the kidnappers wouldn't take a very good view of us," said Rollison. "How is Mary, by the way?"

"Practically herself," Adrian Bell answered. "She asked me to go and see her, and gave me the gist of what has happened and asked me to come and talk to you. *You're* very much on the defensive," went on Bell. "And I really would keep everything off the record until you approved release of the story." When Rollison made no comment, he continued, resignedly: "At least, call on me if I can help." He became a boy again. "I've been a Toffophile since I can remember, I must have read all there is to read about you. I think you're one of the nation's greats!" Still boyishly, he laughed and went on: "Can you tell me this: did the McGees come to you for urgent help?"

"Yes. Surely Mary told you."

"Mary tells me just as much as she wants to," Adrian replied drily.

"Did you in fact tell Mary a great deal about me before she came to see me?"

"Heaps, I've a cuttings book about you, collected over the years, and I lent it to Mary and her sisters," answered Adrian in turn. "But I couldn't be sure whether they wanted help or a scalp! Are you worried about Jolly?"

The question was slipped in so casually that Rollison was on the point of saying: "Yes." But he stopped himself. Adrian Bell might be wholly trustworthy, but if the news were worthwhile, he might also fall to the lure of a front-page story. So, he compromised.

"If he were missing, I would be," Rollison said.

Across his words, quite loudly, came a cry; a woman's sharp cry of protest. He swung round and strode towards the front door. Outside there was a microphone as well as a mirror, and the cry had been magnified by that. With young Bell at his heels, he glanced up at the mirror.

There, a youth and a woman were struggling, and beyond them, halfway up the top flight of stairs of the house, came another man. Rollison pulled open the door, planning to get between man and girl who was in urgent need of help, but as it opened, an almost unbelievable thing happened. The youth on the landing went hurtling down the stairs, and the young woman stood breathing hard but apparently unhurt.

Was this Rose Sapelli? She must be! Wonderful, wonderful Rose Sapelli!

The man who had been coming up the stairs flattened himself against the wall. The falling youth grabbed at the banister rail, missed, grabbed at the man, missed, and went crashing onto the half-landing. As he fell, Rollison pushed past Rose Sapelli, rasped: "Wait inside," and rushed down the stairs.

The man who was flattened against the wall snatched a knife from his pocket. The blade glinted. It looked long, thin, deadly. He raised his hand to slash with it, as if thinking that Rollison could not stop his downward plunge in time to save himself from being wounded. What he had not bargained for was the way Rollison leapt from one of the stairs and hurtled bodily at him, crashing into him before the knife could fall. They went down, together, Toff on top and assailant underneath, and they crashed down on the youth, who had made no attempt to get up. The knife fell, struck the wall, clattered, and bumped from stair to stair. And as it landed and the Toff took breath, the Toff watched it.

Beyond the cruel blade of steel, he saw another man; a third man, here.

In the third man's hand was an automatic pistol, levelled at him. A thin finger was on the trigger. If he squeezed, he could not fail to hit. In a voice so steady it surprised even him, Rollison said:

"I shouldn't. Murder means life and life's a long time."

CHAPTER IX

Long Time . . .

'Life' was a long time.

The man covered Rollison, and did not move; and although it was only a few seconds, that seemed a lifetime.

Rollison, sprawled on top of two visitors and staring at the third, tried desperately to think of any way to dodge a bullet or to overcome the man with the gun. Suddenly, a way opened up for him, for the man underneath gave a great heave, to free himself. Rollison could have resisted this by thrusting himself down, but instead he helped, allowing himself to be flung towards the wall. Both the others sprang towards the lower stairs—and then seemed to freeze at the sight of the gun.

All Rollison had to do was push one, and he went flying towards the third man.

What Rollison hadn't expected was the shot. It roared in the close confines of the stair well, and the bullet must have struck the youth who had sprung up from beneath him; the one he had stopped. For the youth began to sink to the stairs, very slowly, crumpling up almost as if he were being folded by invisible hands. Then, the man with the gun spun round and ran down the stairs.

Adrian Bell called out in a hoarse voice: "Stop him!"

"You won't stop him by standing there," Rose Sapelli said, and disgust rang in her voice. "Get out of my way, or—"

She broke off, undoubtedly because of Rollison's sudden movement. Rollison placed his hands on the railing, and swung himself over, into the well. If he let go he would fall past the three steep flights onto thinly covered concrete below; but he didn't slip. The man with the gun had turned the curve in the stairs and was halfway down the next flight when Rollison's legs and feet loomed in front of him, feet catching him in the chest. He fell back as if pole-axed, and there was a loud crack as the back of his head struck the edge of a stair. Rollison used the banister rails to steady himself, and landed lightly on his feet. By that time Rose Sapelli was on the landing outside Rollison's flat, above the unconscious man, with Adrian Bell just behind her. There was no sign of the one whom Rose had flung down the stairs.

She glanced at Rollison.

No one could doubt the almost passionate warmth of approval in her expression, and it made her whole face radiant. And she was *beautiful*. Her hair was dark and glossy, her skin an olive-brown, her lips were a joy to see. In a split second of time, while she looked at him, he had a sense of shock: bewilderment; wonderment. And then in her matter of fact voice, with its Cockney intonation at variance with her exotic appearance, she said:

"Better get him upstairs, hadn't we?"

"Yes. I'll take his legs—"

"You do nothing of the sort. Here, you," she went on, turning to Adrian Bell. "Do something for your living, go and pick up this sonofabitch's legs. You come up, Mr. Rollison, you'll run yourself into the ground if you keep on. And watch that little basket in your flat."

Meekly, Adrian did what he was told.

As meekly, Rollison went up, squeezing close to the wall, past Rose who now appeared to ignore him, then past Adrian who waited to let him pass. The second of the men on whom Rollison had fallen wasn't in sight: could he have escaped in the shemozzle, Rollison wondered? Then he saw him standing just inside the flat, looking dazed. He moistened his lips, cringed back as Rollison drew level, and muttered :

"Don't let that bitch get at me !"

"Come on," Rollison said, gripping his arm, twisting him round and thrusting him towards the trophy wall. The man—no more than a youth—stumbled against a chair and nearly fell. "Come on," repeated Rollison roughly. "Who are you? Who are you from?"

He sensed that if he pressed hard enough now this frightened youth might crack. He sensed something else; he had taken a lot out of himself in that short, sharp burst of action, and needed to relax. There was no chance to. The youth had thin, fair, curly hair, high cheekbones, tiny eyes, wide-spaced teeth showing because he was breathing through his lips. His nose was tip-tilted so that his nostrils showed dark; about that, about everything, there was something quite repellent.

"I'm—I'm Fred Tidy." The words seemed to choke him.

Rollison gripped him by the shoulders and shook him to and fro, let him go and stagger into the chair.

"*Who sent you?*" he demanded, thrusting his face close to the youth's.

The youth began to speak, spluttered, closed his mouth, tried again and gasped :

"I came to stop Jimmy." Before Rollison could move or speak, he went on as if he couldn't get the words out fast enough. "Pat told Jimmy it was easy, there was a pony in it for him if he helped to put you away. I—I didn't want him to get into no more trouble. Is—is—is he okay?"

Jimmy, obviously, was the man who had been shot. Something of Rollison's reaction must have shown in his face, for the man in his grasp suddenly raised his voice and screamed :

"*Is he okay?*"

"He was hurt," Rollison replied. "I don't know how badly."

"That shot—" the youth began.

In a very gentle voice from behind him, Rose Sapelli said : "I'm afraid he's dead."

Rollison, startled, turned to look at her. She was staring at the youth, who made no attempt to free himself, but stood motionless, mouth open, eyes rounded. Slowly, very slowly, tears began to well up in his eyes; slowly, his shoulders began to heave and his mouth to pucker, and he began to cry. Rollison let him go, and looked helplessly at Rose, who raised a hand at him in a kind of reassurance.

"Let him cry, it will do him good," she said, and then she gave a funny little snort of a laugh. "We've got other problems, Mr. Rollison." She turned and pointed towards the hallway, which was part lounge, for guests with time on their hands.

One man was stretched out on a couch; the man who had fired the shot. He was absolutely motionless, and a dread thought entered Rollison's head.

"He's not dead, too?"

"Shouldn't think so," said Rose in her unbelievably matter-of-fact voice. "He hit his head an almighty crack, though, and his pulse is sub-normal. We'd better have a doctor, quick."

"Yes. Where is the dead man?"

"Left him on the stairs," Rose answered. "No sense in moving a corpse, the cops would think you'd done it to hide something." She gave a little, sultry smile, somehow intensely personal. "Especially it being you ! Will you call the police?"

"Yes," Rollison promised.

"Anything else you need me for?"

"What will you do if I say 'no'?" asked Rollison.

"Look after that poor kid behind you," replied Rose.

All the time they had been talking there had been a

stifled crying, and now Rollison glanced round, to see tears spilling down the youth's cheeks; he seemed to have given himself up to an orgy of grief, and be oblivious to Rose and the Toff.

"Why not take him into the kitchen," Rollison suggested.

"You mean I'm going to find out where the kitchen is at last?" asked Rose, with that slightly tart humour. "Show me." She added "please" as an afterthought.

He led her along the passage past the bedrooms and Jolly's room to the spacious kitchen, which still looked spick and span. There was plenty of room, and a wooden armchair which Jolly sat in when looking through newspapers. *Jolly*. Fear for him stabbed through Rollison, together with a surge of self-reproach. He seemed to be doing everything but look for Jolly.

"This will do fine," decided Rose. "I'll see to the boy, no need for you to worry."

She went into the big room the way she had come, while Rollison went the other way, towards the hall. He saw Adrian Bell, sideways on and looking down; Bell did not appear to notice him, but he stirred when Rollison drew close and asked in a muted voice :

"Is *he* dead, too?"

"Have you tried his pulse?"

"I—er—no."

"Tell you what you can do," said Rollison briskly. "Telephone Scotland Yard and see if Superintendent Grice is in. You'll find a telephone in there."

He pointed to the big room.

Bell went off, as if glad there was some way he could help, and Rollison knelt by the side of the unconscious man, but he did not feel his pulse. He began to run through the pockets of his braided, waisted jacket and his tight, washed-out jeans. In the wallet there were a few pound notes and a credit card and odds and ends. It was a Medway's bank card. You never could tell. If this card was his, he was Patrick Kidd. There was nothing

else. In the slit pockets of the tight-fitting jacket there
were bus tickets, some keys and some loose change; in the
hip pocket of the jeans, a handkerchief. It was easy to
move him about because he was very thin, but apart from
the name 'Patrick Kidd' there seemed nothing worth
finding.

In the slanting front pocket of the jeans was an
envelope, folded several times. When Rollison straightened
it out he saw it was addressed to *Patrick Kidd, Esq.* But
there was no street name. It was empty, but on one corner
was a telephone number, all figures but giving him a
clue : this was the Whitechapel Exchange.

He slipped this into his pocket, and checked the other's
wallet again. He found a small, coloured snapshot of a
pretty girl with long legs in long pants. He turned it over
and saw a rubber stamp impression : *McGee's Staff Photo
Service.*

Did this girl work at McGee's?

He put it with the paper, and, at last felt the pulse in
a thin, unexpectedly graceful wrist. The skin was so fair
and the size so small it could almost have been a girl's
and Rollison could practically see the tiny finger on the
trigger.

Well, this was no girl !

He straightened up and went into the big room, where
Adrian Bell was putting down the receiver. He said with
gloomy satisfaction : "Grice is on his way. They wouldn't
give him a message until they knew it was from you. That
worked like a charm." He looked down at the prisoner,
frowning. "He any better?"

"No." Rollison picked up the receiver and rang the
Whitechapel number, as he asked : "Did you say we
needed a doctor?"

Adrian looked at him broodingly, and answered after
what seemed a long time, and with great deliberation.

"Yes. I do sometimes keep my wits about me. I know
I haven't exactly covered myself with glory and I also

know that I am a physical coward. It is one of my great
drawbacks and as a newspaperman I ought to do better.
However, I usually recover—get my second wind, so to
speak—and I shall be all right."

"I don't know what you're talking about." The number
was ringing but there was no answer.

"Ask the young and beautiful Amazon," said Bell, with
a touch of bitterness. "One question, if I may."

"Carry on." Rollison put down the receiver.

"Is this shindy off the record?" asked Adrian Bell.

"You know what happened but you don't know why,
so there isn't the slightest reason why you shouldn't tell
your news editor. I'd rather you kept it separate from
the McGee business for the time being, at least. It's
probably connected but there's no certainty about that."
As Rollison spoke, he saw Bell's eyes light up, and as he
finished, the young man reached the telephone.

A kind of miracle happened: in his voice, in his
manner, in his choice of words.

"News Desk . . . Adrian Bell . . . Ready . . . Richard
Rollison, the Toff, attacked in his Mayfair apartment less
than an hour ago, in fact at 2.30 . . . Yes . . . One man
dead, shot dead, killer caught and unconscious. Third
man . . . sorry, assailant . . . also held. Yard's Superintendent Grice is on his way. I'm sticking . . . Give me
that back, will you? . . Oh, and add that I am talking
from Rollison's study, staring at his trophy wall."

Rollison was almost laughing, although there was
nothing to laugh about, and—there was no news of
Jolly.

Grice would be here in a very few minutes and that
would mean more delay. He went into the kitchen, where
the young man was in the chair, rocking to and fro with
abject misery, and Rose was at the sink, washing up after
Rollison's snack lunch. She glanced round. He hadn't
realised before what a figure she had.

"The dead man's his brother," she announced. "Any

hope of preventing the cops from taking him?"

"You can try to persuade them," Rollison said. "Say I said it would probably be the best thing." He took out the photograph and spoke sharply to the youth. "Do you know this girl?"

The other focused his gaze, but needed only a single glance, before he muttered :

"She—she used to go with Pat, then they had a row."

"Do you know where she lives?"

"No," Fred Tidy replied. "She—she works at McGee's, she—"

He was overcome by another fit of crying, and Rollison put the picture away as Rose asked sharply :

"Where are *you* going?"

"To look for Jolly," Rollison answered. "I'll be back or will telephone as soon as I can."

She turned, to face him, a glass in one hand and a knife in the other; and she said with deep feeling :

"Oh, *do* find him!"

"I'll find him," he said, and was gone.

He slipped along the main passage and out of the front door, unseen by Adrian Bell, whose voice still droned into the telephone. There were a few coins, a bunch of keys and a bicycle chain on the stairs; Rollison scooped up the keys and dropped them into his pocket, but left the rest for the police. He reached the front door, which was open, and stepped into the street. A police car might appear at any moment, Grice wouldn't lose a minute. Several cars were moving about, two were double-parked, people were on either side of the street. He saw no police vehicle. A taxi pulled in a few yards along and he strode towards it as an elderly woman got out, and, on the pavement, began to fumble with her handbag for change. He stood near but not near enough to crowd her, hoping that he was concealed.

A police car swung round the corner.

Rollison ducked below the level of the square roof of

the taxi. The elderly woman produced not change but a fifty pence piece. The police car passed and pulled in outside Number 25. Rollison said: "May I?" and slipped into the cab as the driver was giving change.

"Thank you, driver. Here's a shilling."

"Thank *you*, madam." The driver turned to look at Rollison, one eyebrow raised; soon the second eyebrow joined the first; obviously he recognised his new fare. "Where to, sir?" He looked pointedly into his driving mirror, obviously at the police car.

"Do you know Elm Avenue, Knightsbridge?"

"Just behind Harrods, yes."

"Drop me at the corner, will you?" asked Rollison.

"Okay, sir."

Okay. A near-crying boy, a desperate voice: "Is he okay?" Back there, he was still crying for his dead brother.

Rollison settled back. In spite of that last thought, he was feeling better. He had slipped the police and could do a lot of things before Grice told him not to! And he was in action, knowing exactly what he wanted to do next.

First: search the flat at Elm Avenue, where Marie said she had come from.

The drive through thick traffic and brilliant sunshine which gave an illusion of warmth, took twenty minutes. He tipped the cabby generously and walked along Elm Avenue. It was a short, dead-end street. All the houses, four in two terraces, had pillared porches, and all but two or three houses were freshly painted white. Here was Knightsbridge and prosperity. He walked along to Number 11, noticing half a dozen bells in some of the porches. So much of this prosperity was illusory, there were many flats and flatlets here.

On the side of the porch of Number 11, there were six; and above the top bell was a card on which was printed in block capitals: MCGEE. He tried the front door, but it was locked. He took out a knife with a steel blade of great tensile strength, and inserted it between the door and the frame. It took some time, but no one had come near when the lock clicked back. He opened the door and stepped into the wide hall, which divided into staircase and passage at the far end. Tall, white-painted doors were on one side, there were two more at the head of the first flight of stairs, two at the next landing. The house was very quiet, not even traffic noises penetrated.

The door at the end of the landing was marked : *McGee*.

Was this Marie's flat? Or Maria's? Or a family *pied-à-terre?* In a very few minutes he should find out, for this lock was easier to force than the one downstairs. He used a slender pick-lock, and soon the lock clicked back. He waited, for the snap of sound seemed to echo so loudly. No one appeared, nothing happened. He turned the handle and pushed open the door, and there was still no sound. He stepped into a large and beautifully furnished room, bright from the sunlight, with traffic murmuring from a long way off.

Almost in front of the door was a large photograph of a McGee girl. He wasn't sure which one it was, but was sure of the large, black lettering across the top of the photograph. The words were simple : *Dead*—£000. *Alive*—£100,000.

CHAPTER X

Ransom

Rollison stood stockstill in front of the photograph. It was at least twenty inches by twelve, and a beautiful reproduction; yet there was something sinister in the lettering, done with a felt pen. *Dead*—£000. *Alive*—£100,000. Had one of the sisters been taken away, since Mary's return? Had the gunman been sent to make sure that he, the Toff, couldn't help? He went close and scrutinised the picture. There were no fingerprints; they would have shown up at once on the glossy surface.

He began to search the flat.

There was this large room, a smaller bedroom, bathroom and kitchen, all beautifully appointed. He soon had one answer: only one person lived here. There was one double bed, a variety of personal things. Marie's? He found jewellery in unlocked drawers, brooches, rings, bracelets and earrings. He held a ring up to the light and had no shadow of doubt that it was of real diamonds and emeralds. He ran his hands lightly over silken and nylon lingerie and stockings, but found nothing where he had half-expected to find a gun. He opened the bottom drawer of a chest of drawers and found two wads of five pound notes, flipped them through his fingers and guessed there were £250 in each. Who but a McGee would be so careless with diamonds and gems and good new money?

There must be ten thousand poundsworth here, in all, and whoever had left the photograph had left it here and gone off demanding the fortune. He found no clue to the girl's identity, but in the big room a writing desk was full of letters addressed to Miss Marie McGee.

Absently, he glanced at one.

My dearest, darling . . .

It was a love letter, of course. He put it back in the envelope, and then stared at the pile of letters. There were dozens, perhaps hundreds! And seven or eight were unopened. Each seemed to be addressed in a different hand : Good God! Love letters by the hundred, so many that the McGee girl who lived here had not even troubled to open them all.

He stood back.

It was possible that the kidnapper was one of the men who had written these letters. If the police were handling this enquiry they would have to check each name and see each writer.

He hadn't time; and it wasn't his way.

He finished the search, and found nothing else of interest, except a telephone and address book. He glanced down the telephone list and saw Whitechapel 43222. His heart missed a beat, for this was the number scrawled on the envelope in his pocket, which he had tried to call.

The address book might come in useful, and he slipped it into his pocket. He couldn't be sure, had no idea what his next step would be. He went across to the photograph and studied the face. Marie was smiling slightly; was dimpled slightly; and had a most provocative and yet demure look.

Where was she?

Find Marie, he wondered with a sudden stab of revelation, and find Jolly? They might possibly be imprisoned in the same place; the only way to know was to find one or the other.

Anyone who came to the flat after him would know that the lock had been forced, but he had left no clues that he had been there. He stood on the porch, looking up and down; the only people in sight had their backs to him, collars turned up, although it was not so cold. He thought he saw a face at the window of the house opposite but couldn't be sure, the sunlight shone so brightly on the window. He went towards the end of the street, where traffic was milling, a dozen motorists were hunting for parking places while traffic wardens were having a field day and the parking meters looked like the bars of a prison. No taxi was in sight.

He walked briskly towards Knightsbridge itself. Had he come in one of his own cars he would have been picked up by the police in a moment, for he had no doubt that Grice had sent or would soon send out a call for him. A taxi with its hire sign alight turned out of a side street, and five minutes later he was at Globe Crescent, Chelsea.

Here, the leaves were russet brown underfoot and the branches were bare, like skeletons, and across the river Battersea Power Station towered, visible from the street. He turned into the house from which Mary had come only a few hours ago, carried in a most indecorous way. As he reached the door it opened and a fur-coated, bare-headed woman appeared, leading a Yorkshire terrier.

It yapped.

"Quiet, Fidel," she said, without any firmness at all. "Good afternoon."

"Good afternoon."

Fidel not only yapped but struggled to get at Rollison's trousers.

"Be quiet, Fidel. Were you coming to see me?"

"If you are Miss McGee—" began Rollison.

A frosty look appeared in the woman's eyes. She was a well-preserved, not unattractive sixty, Rollison judged, who did not approve of Miss McGee.

"She is on the second floor," she stated. "*Good* after-noon."

The Yorkshire terrier, sensing her disapproval, went back into a positive frenzy of yapping and struggling, long wavy hair dancing as if in a high wind. His mistress no longer pretended to rebuke him but swept past.

Rollison went in, and closed the street door.

He walked up two flights of narrow stairs; in every way this house was smaller and narrower than 11 Elm Avenue, and found a door marked in gilt lettering on a painted shield patterned, if he were not mistaken, like a tin of soup. He knocked and rang but no one answered. He rang again, wondering why the woman had been so disapproving. There was still no answer, so he took out his skeleton key. In a moment he was inside, closing the door behind him.

Placed on an old oak chair, facing the door, was a copy of the photograph that had been at the other flat. The wording was different, that was all :

Want her back? it ran. £100,000—*and cheap at the price.*

Rollison examined this as he had the other, soon sure it contained no fingerprints. He began to search this flat in turn. It had several pleasant rooms, one of them overlooking the river. As he searched he kept looking out; the sun was so bright, a few fir trees gave a cloak of green, the dead fairylights of the Battersea Pleasure Gardens glistened as if the sun were lighting them better than electric current. Barges passed : and a police launch, one of the crew standing and dipping into the water.

There seemed nothing of significance anywhere here.

A few love letters from three different people was about all. No real jewels were loose but some costume jewellery was in a jewel box which was at least as valuable as its contents. There was no address book but by the pale yellow telephone, a list of telephone numbers. He ran his eye down these, and stopped abruptly at Whitechapel 43222.

"So both girls call that number," he remarked aloud; and he took out the envelope taken from the gunman's pocket. There it was . . . 43222.

Should he try it again from here?

He had been lucky so far, and ought not to ride his luck. Luck, he repeated to himself, and then wondered. This place as well as Elm Avenue might be watched, he could not take safety for granted. He looked down into the front garden and onto the road and a crescent-shaped patch of grass and trees between this private drive and the embankment itself, where traffic was moving, very fast, heavy lorries roaring as if this were a race-track. The woman in her mink and the Yorkshire terrier in his fur were in the garden. A flurry of wind stirred leaves and branches, made the dog yap and Rollison shiver.

He went down and walked briskly towards King's Road, away from the Embankment, and for the first time, thought he was being followed. He turned right, into narrow streets built long ago, part of the Chelsea where Benjamin Franklin had plotted against the King. There was a warren of these narrow streets, and he easily doubled back.

He *was* being followed.

A small man had been behind him; a natty man, too, wearing a dark overcoat, a red and white muffler and a bowler. From behind, he was almost a caricature of Jolly. Rollison dodged into a narrow doorway as the man doubled back. As he passed, Rollison caught a glimpse of a sharp, pointed nose, a sharp pointed chin, and high cheekbones. The man did not look into the doorway and when he was safely past, Rollison stepped out and up to him getting so close that by stretching out a hand, he could grip the other's shoulder. They were halfway along a street perhaps fifty yards from end to end.

Rollison said, sharply : "Don't move."

The man jumped so wildly that it almost seemed deliberate—and in the same movement he spun round. Rollison had seldom seen a man move more quickly, nor seen a sharper glint in deepset eyes. Half-prepared, he

chopped the back of his hand down onto a wrist stretched
out towards him, prehensile-looking, claw-ready for a
grip. Rollison's blow struck home, the man winced, and
on the instant cried:

"Mr. R!"

*The only people who ever called Rollison 'Mr. R.'
were Bill Ebbutt's men.*

Rollison, equally startled, drew back from the attack;
and the other also drew away. He was shaking his head
in baffled bewilderment, and before Rollison could speak,
he said complainingly:

"Been chasing you all over London, I have, and what
happens? You catch me from behind, and scare the living
daylight out of me. You're a perishing marvel, Mr. R,
that's what you are."

"And who are you and why follow me?" asked Rollison,
still wary.

The man put a hand to his inside pocket, making him
feel warier still, but all the other brought out was an
envelope. Instantly, Rollison recognised Bill Ebbutt's
spidery handwriting. This was addressed to him, Rollison,
and as he took it he saw on the reverse side:

This introduces Bony William, Mr. R. You can trust
him.

"*Bony* William?" asked Rollison, almost incredulously.

"That's me," the little man said. "I got the car, Mr. R,
wouldn't we be warmer sitting in it? This wind's perishing."

It was howling along the narrow street; when they
drew within sight of the river, the surface was whipped
up to waves that seemed two feet high. Bony William led
the way to a roomy old Ford, and opened the driving
door.

"Your side," said Rollison.

"Not a bit of it, Bill said you might want some transport, Mr. R. Bit of luck, I can tell you—I was coming into Gresham Terrace when you was getting into the cab. You fooled the coppers, but you have to get up very early to fool me!"

Rollison made appropriate comments, and opened the letter. Inside, the message was typed. There were seven names and addresses, and four had telephone numbers opposite.

"These chaps are okay," Ebbutt had written. "Ask Bony about them."

Bony was already telling him.

"Mick Carter can crack any crib Chubb ever created," he declared, "but he's a bit rusty. You once saved his brother from coming a cropper . . ."

Brother. Jimmy Tidy, Fred Tidy. "It's his brother."

". . . Tiger Simms, you know Tiger, he's just a strong-arm boy," stated Bony. "John Sharples, now, he's a cat-burglar; *and* in practice. Do any job from any roof or drainpipe. You could have shopped him once, but you didn't. Then there's number 4, who's okay—"

"Is he okay?"

"Lenny the Link," went on Bony William. "Had the Fraud Squad after him for years, he has, and knows more about millionaires than anyone else Bill knows! Memory like an elephant's. Don't ask him to do anything, though, he's as blind as a bat. And then there's number 5, that's Benbow."

There was no need for Bony to say who Benbow was, for Benbow had a great following in the East End, although most people wondered why. He was the leader of a gang of near-hooligans who often threatened trouble but in fact made very little. He could be relied on to stop a riot and almost always seemed to be in the middle of one. What earned him the loyalty of so many it was hard to say, but he was as good as a Pied Piper when a crowd was needed in a hurry. He had one other rare ability, too; he could spirit wanted men and women away, especially when the heat was on from the police.

"Need anything else?" enquired Bony of Rollison.

"Not yet, at all events," Rollison answered, feeling positively overwhelmed. "How will you get home?"

"Tube," answered Bony. He opened the passenger door, jumped out and bounded along the pavement towards the Embankment in an effort to beat the cold.

Now, Rollison had others to help and a car no one would dream was his.

He sat back for a few moments, thinking . . .

And again, quite suddenly, he knew exactly what to do next.

He got out, put enough money in the meter by the car to ensure that it would last until parking hours were over, and walked back to Number 3. The front door was unlocked and this time he encountered no one. He went up to the flat from which Mary had been abducted, and rang the bell, but there was no sound or response, so he picked the lock again. Now the sun had fallen and the room seemed very dark. He went straight to the address book and checked : Maria.

There she was : Maria, 61 Emblem Court, Mayfair. He made a mental note of that and jotted down the telephone number—81325. Then he sat so that he faced the door, and dialled the Whitechapel number, but again there was no reply. He tried the number of his own flat, and almost at once a man and a woman answered—a gruff-voiced man, almost certainly a policeman.

"Mr. Rollison's residence," the woman said, and she sounded like Rose, in anger.

"This is Mayfair 85712," the man said. "Can I help you?"

"Is Mr. Grice there?" Rollison asked sharply.

"Who wants him?" enquired the man.

"Mr. Rollison!" Rose cried, obviously from the kitchen extension. "Don't come back or the cops will—"

A man roared : "Keep quiet !"

"Mr. Grice!" another called.

"Little *bitch*," growled someone else, *sotto voce*.

"If you touch me I'll break your fat neck." Rose's voice was nearly a snarl. "I'll charge you with assault, that's what I'll do. I want to talk to Mr. Rollison."

"Well, you can't!" A moment's silence was followed by a gasp and what sounded like a crash, as if the kitchen rocking chair had toppled over. Then, breathless but quite calmly, Rose Sapelli spoke again.

"If you're still there, Mr. Rollison, don't let Grice or anyone else fool you. If you come they'll clap you in clink. They've taken the kid already. I'm here on me own but Bill's sending some company, so I'll be all right. Best of luck, sir."

Before Rollison could speak, before he fully realised that Rose had finished, another voice came on the line, the unmistakable voice of Superintendent William Grice of the Criminal Investigation Department of New Scotland Yard.

"If you don't come over at once, Mr. Rollison, you won't need luck, you'll need a miracle." He was very precise and almost curt, and what he said told Rollison two things. First, that someone else who mattered was in the flat, he wouldn't have used the formal 'Mr. Rollison' otherwise. Second, that for some reason it was hard to understand, Grice really thought he was in trouble.

CHAPTER XI

How Serious?

"Bill," said Rollison in a mild voice, "come off it."

"I am very serious indeed," Grice asseverated.

"Take it from me," interpolated Rose from the extension, "they're after you."

Rollison was already convinced that Grice was serious, but he did not understand why. What could make the police want him so badly? The death of the man on the stairs wasn't remotely his fault, and at least two witnesses could say so. Even if the police thought Rose's evidence suspect, they could hardly doubt Adrian Bell's. These things flashed through his mind with the speed of sound; so did the fact that he had been in grievous trouble with the police often before, but he had always known why.

"My strong advice to you," said Grice, "is to come to your flat at once."

Without a pause, Rollison asked: "Do you know what's happened about Jolly?"

"I know that you say he's been kidnapped," Grice answered. "I want to know why, I want to know everything you are keeping back, and I want to know where Marie McGee is."

"Marie *McGee*!" exploded the Toff.

"Don't pretend that you don't know she is missing for several hours," Grice said. "Wherever you are, come here at once."

Before Rollison could speak again, he rang off.

Rollison put down the receiver sharply, feeling very much on edge. Nothing moved in the flat or seemed to move outside. He uncrossed his legs, and then looked at the haphazard typing of Bill Ebbutt's letter. He ran his finger along the line of Lenny the Link, who had a Bethnal Green number, and dialled it. Whatever else Grice did, he must not make him, Rollison, lose any time. The dialling tone rang on and on until he thought there would be no answer, but at last there was a break, and a man said in a rather gentle, patient-sounding voice:

"This is Leonard Links."

"Mr. Links," began Rollison. "This is—"

"Do permit me to show off a little, Mr. Rollison," said the other man. "I recognised your voice on the first syllable. I am very glad to speak to you again." Again? "In case you don't remember it was seventeen years ago when you were interested in some fraudulent share certification." Links laughed, as if at his own audacity, and said: "How can I help you, sir?"

Rollison recovered in time to ask at once: "Can you tell me who the subscriber is on Whitechapel 43222? That would be a great help."

There was a pause, before Links answered: "I've heard the number, yes." Rollison's heart missed a beat, only to droop when the other went on: "I cannot get instant recall on it, Mr. Rollison. Is there a number where I can call you when I do remember?"

"I'll have to call you," replied Rollison.

"Oh, dear. I hope that isn't as ominous as it sounds. Can Bill Ebbutt—"

"I've all the help I need," Rollison assured him. "Try hard to recall that subscriber, won't you?"

"I will indeed," promised Lenny the Link, and rang off.

Rollison put the receiver down firmly, and considered. He had planned to send the girls to Old Glory's, but after the shooting he was less inclined to do that; and there was an alternative hiding place in the East End—not far from one of the McGee factories. He rang Benbow's number, in Millwall, and this time the reply came almost as soon as the ringing sound. A man with a very deep, very resonant voice, said:

"Benbow."

"Richard Rollison," stated the Toff.

Not sounding even slightly out of countenance, Benbow asked:

"How can I help you, Toff?"

"I may want to store some packages for a few days," Rollison said. "Can you do that for me so that they can't be traced and at the same time can't be hurt?"

Without a pause, Benbow responded: "Will they want bed and board?"

"Yes."

"Can they share a room?"

"Yes."

"Bring them to me well wrapped up," said Benbow without a moment's hesitation. "Do you know where to find me, Toff?"

"If you're still aboard the *Arrow*, yes."

"That's where you'll find me to my dying day," declared Benbow. "Have you yet had news about Jolly?"

"No," answered Rollison, and the very thought seemed to choke him.

"There's nothing I won't do to help that man," Benbow assured him. "Nothing, Mr. R."

It was on the tip of the Toff's tongue to ask why, but there was little time, so all he said was simply: "That goes for me, too." He rang off first, this time.

It was quite dark, now. The only lights outside were from street-lamps and lamps on the river, reflected in the high waves, and four cars going fast along the Embankment. What time was it? The luminous dial of his watch showed that it was nearly six o'clock. Could he expect Mary back yet? As he wondered he realised a remarkable thing: he had not given a second thought to Grice's 'order' or Rose's warning. He had just taken it for granted that he shouldn't go home, yet he needed to know why Grice, more friend than enemy for over twenty-five years, had spoken so ominously.

He got up and went to the kitchen; acutely aware that he had eaten so little at lunch; and remembering Jolly. He closed the door before putting on the light, found some apples and milk in the small refrigerator and, in a larder, nearly a whole, very rich fruit cake. He bit into the cake and found it rich in flavour. Could Mary McGee cook like this? He ate, sipped, ate, sipped, finished, and then put out the light and stepped into the main part of the flat.

He had timed it well, for a key was turning in the lock. Voices sounded faintly, then became louder; obviously the door had opened.

". . . c-c-can say is that I made a b-b-big mistake," Mary McGee was saying. Her voice was most attractive and the stammer added to the appeal. "I-I-I sh-shouldn't have held out against telling p-p-poppa!"

Whoever was with her made no reply. There was a click and a light went on; another as of a closing door, and then a gasp; silence, and Maria's unmistakable voice, Maria's unmistakable venom.

"They've been here too," she said. "I could cut their throats!"

Obviously they had seen the photograph, with its demand; as they must have seen the one in the other flat. Now Rollison shifted his position so that he could see them both. They stood in front of the photograph, backs to the door, and they might have been identical twins. They wore ponchos in vivid colours, with green and yellow predominating, the skirts beneath so short that the corners of the ponchos dropped inches lower. Their faces were almost identical.

"Well," Rollison said, "that's a change for the better, even if I feel a little rueful. Punishment for a spanking desexing. Punishment for kidnapping sister, a cut throat.

How are you both?"

They were amazed; they swivelled towards him and gaped, Maria at least as startled and off-balance as her sister. He beamed on them; and the light fell in such a way as to accentuate his already remarkable good looks. He moved towards the door and their eyes and bodies seemed to turn towards him; all he did was turn the key in the lock and slip it into his pocket.

"So you should have told poppa," he said.

"Y-y-yes," answered Mary, almost tearful. "He would have paid, and we wouldn't have been in th-th-this mess. Can't *you* do something to help?"

"He couldn't help pussy!" said Maria, thinly.

The almost grotesque fact was that she somehow looked ugly. Her appearance had to do with the twist of her lips and a tension at her nose and the expression in her eyes. She looked as if she hated him. He had a sharp sense that she might throw herself at him, bodily, and that if she did, Mary would help her. So he held up his right hand, palm outwards.

"I can help," he said as if on oath.

"You wouldn't lift a finger, you're too fond of that old man!"

"Maria," Rollison said softly, "I know we've got off on the wrong foot, but I won't find Jolly any quicker by leaving you to the lions. Do you really want my help? Or have I put myself beyond the pale?"

"Oh, we w-w-want it!" cried Mary. "Don't we, Maria! Now p-p-poppa's away, we must have help to find Marie, we absolutely m-m-must! And the Toff d-d-*did* rescue me, he really d-d-did, if it hadn't been for him goodness knows what would have happened to m-m-me."

All this time, her sister was studying the Toff, and the light of venom seemed to have faded from her eyes, the tension lines eased from her mouth. Instead of being ugly, she looked very, very beautiful. There was more character in her face than in Mary's, who looked what she seemed to be: a pleasant young woman of remarkable charm.

"Toff," Maria asked, "how could you help?"

"By preventing anyone from kidnapping either of you."

"How?"

"By hiding you."

"Where?"

"If you don't know you can't tell anybody."

"Oh, p-p-*please!*" breathed Mary. "Please h-h-hide us!"

"And what would you do while we were in hiding?" asked Maria, still very wary. Something seemed to have happened to her figure: she was more seductive, more sensuous-looking: as if some magic conjuror had poured some aphrodisiac into her while they had been standing here.

"Find Marie," he answered.

"How?" demanded Maria.

"I would need to play it by ear," Rollison said. "Probably I would have to buy her back."

"*You* buy her!" cried Mary. "Oh, how w-w-wonderful! Do you really mean it? Could—c-c-could you afford it?"

"Even if you could afford a hundred thousand pounds, why should you, for us?" asked Maria. Her voice was much gentler now, and she moved forward.

Rollison watched her warily, not at all sure that he could trust her, even though her lips, her eyes, her body and her mood all seemed to be melting. He was sure that he needed them on his side, and he felt certain that if he asked too many questions they would be evasive. His first task was to convince them that he took the situation at its face value, although he was full of doubt; his second, to convince them that he was serious.

"Not for you," he said calmly. "For Jolly."

"Maria!" cried Mary. "He means it, he really does!"

"Can you put your hands on a hundred thousand pounds?" demanded Maria.

"What I don't have I could easily borrow," Rollison retorted. "What happens when one or the other of you is—ah—kidnapped? Who acts as go-between?" Although he asked the question soberly, it was hard to believe the subject was serious; hard to believe that these girls were under such threats so often.

"Poppa fixes it!" cried Mary.

"Daddy arranges it," answered Maria.

"By telephone," said Mary.

"What about your mother?" asked Rollison.

"She has nothing whatever to do with it," declared Maria, sharply. "And she mustn't—do you understand? She mustn't."

"Yes," agreed Rollison. "But why not?"

"That has nothing to do with you, it is simply a family matter. She isn't to be worried, whatever the reason. She—" Maria broke off and seemed to harden again: body, face, eyes, manner. "If you worry her, I'll—"

"Don't start an orgy of threats again," pleaded Rollison. "Supposing your mother needs to know in order to help Marie?"

"She mustn't be worried!" insisted Maria.

"Oh, p-p-*please* don't tell Mummy," pleaded Mary, and tears seemed close to the surface of her eyes. "That's w-w-why—"

"Be quiet!" Maria said with a note of savagery in her voice.

"But I can't be quiet. If he d-d-doesn't know why, how can we expect him to t-t-take any notice of us?" She brushed aside another protest from her sister. "That's why p-p-poppa pays up whenever there's trouble! T-t-to help Mother, to save her from hurt, as well as to help *us*."

"For God's sake stop!" cried Maria in a strangled-sounding voice.

Rollison saw that she was on the raw edge of tension, that she hated all that her sister was saying; he could worry about why later, just as he could come to grips with what they had told him from the beginning, that kidnapping of a McGee girl was a commonplace. Just now, he had to pacify and somehow reassure Maria, and so he went on almost before she had finished.

"It's not important, Maria. Do the kidnappers deal direct with your father, as you said?"

"Yes."

"Now that he's in New York, whom will they contact?"

"One of us, I suppose," Maria said miserably.

"But if you let me hide you, you wouldn't be available to contact, would you? Is there a lawyer, or a friend, or—"

"There's no one," Maria answered starkly. "We always handle it in the family. You're supposed to be so clever, can't you find a third party?"

Rollison said: "Yes. But what would you do if you were left to yourselves?"

"Telephone a man," said Maria, reluctantly.

"Ring Whitechapel 43222!" cried Mary. "And d-d-do whatever the man asks. It's as s-s-simple as th-th-that; it really is. He'll want the m-m-money at a certain place, and when he's got it Marie will be released."

Rollison hid his surge of surprise and satisfaction at hearing the familiar telephone number, and could no longer stop himself from asking with overtones of disbelief:

"How often do these kidnappings really happen?"

"Oh, they've been happening all our lives," said Maria, impatiently. "Ever since we were old enough to walk."

"Oh, b-b-before that!" cried Mary. "My mem-mem-memory's better than yours, I c-c-can remember being stolen from a pram. I really c-c-can. Oh, please help, I can't bear to think of M-M-Marie's being a prisoner anywhere, she's the m-m-most nervous of us all. I g-g-get frightened, but—"

"Will you really hide us and then try to buy Marie back?" Maria asked.

It was so incredible that Rollison almost believed the story; but credible or not, it was more than ever certain that he had to convince them that he believed it, so he promised very simply:

"Yes, I'll hide you."

"Oh, you p-p-pet!" cried Mary.

But it was Maria who moved; Maria of whom he had to be wary. Nevertheless Mary flung her arms round him and put him off his balance, so that he could not have fended Maria off. Even to the last moment he thought she was back to hostility, but as Mary backed away Maria just slid her arms round his neck and pressed against him. The transition came again; her body seemed to be all flesh and yielding, inviting, promising, sweetly demanding: and her lips sought his and she kissed him, her mouth opening slowly, enticingly. Suddenly he had a thought: that no man could resist such a body and such a promise for long; not he, not even Jolly.

Suddenly, she wrenched herself away; and it was like being torn asunder.

"Find her," she breathed. "Find Marie."

"And we'll f-f-forever be g-g-grateful," breathed Mary. Her lips brushed his like a cool salve after burning, and her hands rested and moved about him and then away, as gentle as a butterfly flitting.

"Now," he said in a voice that he himself hardly recognised, "let's go. Pack a few warm clothes and hurry."

Ten minutes later, they were on their way, huddled up in woollens and cloth coats.

Fifty minutes later they were stepping inside Benbow's home, a self-propelled barge near the East India docks. Benbow himself, huge and bearded and as masculine as they were tiny and feminine, took them down into the living quarters of the barge, lit by lamps, to show the garish colours.

"I'll look after them, Toff," he promised. "Don't worry." And he gave a vast grin which seemed to lift ten years from him, and went on in a gargantuan whisper they could not fail to hear : "Whatever you're up to, good luck. But—"

Suddenly his massive hands fell, vice-tight, on Rollison's

shoulders, and he finished into Rollison's ears: "If it's a case of them or Jolly, don't make any mistake—you make it Jolly."

He gripped so hard that he hurt even the Toff.

And then he let go.

CHAPTER XII

"Make it Jolly"

Rollison drove away from the barge, very thoughtful indeed. The noises of the docks made constant background, great cranes were floodlit at the wharfs, whole ships, glimpsed between warehouses and high brick walls, were shown up brightly, men working on them like ants when seen from here. A few tall factories, one of the distant ones new and filled with countless square yellow eyes. McGee's Soups certainly had a factory in this area, and he felt an even greater urge to seek it out. He drove round several streets and saw a big, floodlit sign which was half-hidden by another building. Six or seven lorries thundered past him, and then a stream of cars; of course, it was rush hour.

The cobbles, smeared with the droppings of oil, looked as if they had a shiny streak in the middle. The streetlamps on the walls were old-fashioned, and lit by gas; those on the pavement side were huge concrete posts lit by sodium, making a strange and eerie glow. Rollison moved a few yards, then put his head out of the window and peered up at the sign above the factory.

There it was : *McGee's* Soups.

"Well, I've put the girls close to home," Rollison said to himself wryly. "I wonder how big the factory is. And I wonder if Pat's ex-girl-friend is on this shift."

He turned left, found doors and gates opened and quite suddenly was confronted by a flood of men and women,

all bearing down on him. They came not only from the
main factory but from smaller buildings on one side, and
it seemed that they were not in hundreds but in thousands.

Would he be able to recognise Pat's girl-friend?

The spearhead of the crowd drew close.

"Won't do yourself any good there, mate," a small,
pale-faced man said.

"Git aht while you bloody well can," said a big man
with a strident voice.

But there was no getting out, even if he wished to. The
flood became so great that it seemed almost as if some
would walk straight over the car, but as each group
reached it, they divided, flooding past on either side. Most
ignored him. A few of the younger girls peered in at him.

"My, who let him out?"

"Proper pansy, that one."

"Hi, Charlie Boy!"

He entered into the spirit of this badinage, and soon
won answering smiles. A girl in her teens in the briefest
of hot pants, came along on the other side of the road,
looking across at the car; and he had no doubt at all that
this was the girl of the photograph. Rollison beamed across
at her, and she hesitated, and called:

"Waiting for me, mate?"

"Come on, Edie, he'd eat you!" another girl said.

She had a pert and pretty face and her eyes were very
bright, partly because she had on so much shading and
the eyelashes were so thickly plastered that they looked
like solid black. She had a rosebud of a mouth and a snub
nose, she showed nice but slightly crooked teeth in a smile,
no doubt meant to be seductive; but what struck Rollison
was how *tired* she looked. She still hesitated, and he called
across:

"Does the name Pat mean anything to you?"

She looked startled, and moved across at once, reaching
the side of the car as she said:

"Pat who?"

"Kidd."

"Who wants to know?" she demanded.

"I would like to," Rollison said. "He was hurt this afternoon." He could have added 'arrested', but did not.

"That's too bad," she said, "but me and Pat broke it off a year ago. Don't tell me *he* put you on to me. He doesn't want to see me, does he? Because I don't want to see him."

"No," replied Rollison, gently. "Do you know what he's been doing lately? Who he's been mixing with, for instance."

"Pat? He's a loner," she said. "Too bloody good for the likes of me."

He wanted to know more, but he couldn't keep her standing here, for many of her workmates were whistling at her, or jeering, or grinning. And now she looked both sad and tired.

"Can I take you home?" he suggested, and his eyes gleamed. "Your home!"

"They'd tease the bloody life out of me in the morning," she replied, half-regretfully. "Can't wait to get out of the mad-house, that's what the rush is."

"Mad-house?" asked Rollison quickly.

A couple of middle-aged men, one of them bearded, passed as the word came out. The bearded man said :

"Couldn't use a better word, guv. Come on, Edie !" He gave her a slap on the bottom, and the girl spun round on him, anger roughening her voice.

"You keep your hands to yourself !"

"I could tell you something else you ought to keep to yourself," the bearded man retorted, and roared with laughter.

A few more men and women passed but the stampede was nearly over, most people were walking more sedately. The girl turned back, still muttering resentfully.

"Great big pig, that's what he is."

"Sure I can't take you home?" asked Rollison. If he

could talk to her at leisure he might learn more about the factory, if not Patrick Kidd, and since talking to Mary and Maria, he was very anxious indeed to find out all he could about the McGees.

She hesitated, and then said with a kind of relief in her voice : "Just home, mind."

"Just home," Rollison assured her, and opened the door as she backed away. A moment later she was beside him, long legs stretched out. Now there was room in the road for Rollison to go forward and then reverse; he did so, slowly. The last stragglers appeared to take no notice. He drove to the end of the street, and asked : "Where is home?"

"Tenby Street," she answered.

"Just behind the Blue Dog?"

"That's it," she said, adding in surprise : "You know it?"

"Very well," Rollison told her.

"But you're a swell," she remarked. "A proper toff." She found no significance in the word and he made no attempt to inform her. "Who were you waiting for?"

"I just took a wrong turning," he replied evasively as he turned along the narrow cobbled streets, hundred-year-old, soot-blackened brick warehouses on one side, the mammoth modern factory on the other. Long queues stood at the bus stops, half the men reading evening newspapers, most of the women in cloth coats. A second huge sign on a corner proclaimed : *McGee's Soups*. Just that and no more.

"A wrong turning," she echoed; and sighed. "You can say that again. I wish I'd never seen the place."

"McGee's?"

"What else do you think I mean?" she asked, but there was no real sharpness in her voice.

"Because it's a mad-house?" he prompted, gently.

"Don't get me wrong," she said. "It's okay as factories go. Better than most. We work six-hour shifts and four shifts a day and the lolly's good, but you just have to keep at it. Same bloody thing, day in, day out—*and* to music. And"—he detected an extra note of bitterness in her voice—"I get special treatment, I pick up so much lolly I can't afford to leave. Know what I do?"

"What do you do?"

"I watch the machine that puts the opener on the cans. An inspector, they call me! There's a laugh."

"Edie," said Rollison very quietly, "what's eating you?"

She glanced at him and then stared straight ahead, without answering. He stole a glance at her. There were tears in her eyes, and one trickled slowly down her cheek. She didn't appear to notice. He drove past the front entrance of the huge, brightly-lit factory. A few cars were parked, a few men and women walked down steps leading to the offices, where a more conservative but floodlit sign stretched over the wide doors. The lighted windows in their masses, the floodlight at the front and corners, gave the factory an appearance of some fabulous fairyland.

Absurd?

He found himself at a traffic roundabout where cars and lorries were crowding in from four different main roads. This was going to take time and patience. He had a sense that this girl needed help; another, that she could tell him more about McGees' methods, the plant, the thousands who worked there.

She sniffed; and out of the corner of his eye he saw that she was looking at him again. He edged in between an open greengrocer's cart and a huge, stinking lorry.

"At least it's warm in here," she said.

"Isn't it in the factory?"

"The working conditions are okay," she conceded, the touch of bitterness still there. "It's one hundred per cent hygienic, take it from me! You can get fired for not washing your hands after going to the lav. Oh, you can't blame the *factory*. I just made a bloody fool of myself, that's all."

"May I ask how?" enquired Rollison.

"Mister," she said, "I let Rupert McGee take me for a ride. He likes to treat the factory like a harem, that's what he does. If you're young enough and pretty enough and you've got the kind of curves that catch his eye, then you get invited to a little party. And before you know where you are, you're rolling in the hay. Only it's foam rubber, these days. So you have a good time for a week or two, and then you realise you're not the only one. Sooner or later you get a nice little present and a closed door."

"And what happens if things—" Rollison hesitated, and then added tentatively: "go wrong?"

He moved forward in the traffic jam.

"Go wrong?" She sounded startled; and then suddenly she gave a snort of a laugh. "Don't worry, mister, he looks after all that. And if things go wrong, okay, it's not against the law to have an abortion, is it? Not these days." She brooded before going on: "Don't worry, I'm not in the family way. What happened to me happened to a lot of the others. When you come out of the harem, the rest of the factory knows all about it. No one *respects* you any more. And they all know you get special privileges and you become an inspector which ups the wages by twenty per cent a week. The trouble is, if you live in this part of the world, you've had it. That's what made Pat go sour on me, and I can't say I blame him."

Rollison was torn between recollection that Pat had kept her photograph in spite of what had happened, and thinking of Marie, telling him she and her sisters had been brought up on strange standards; and he thought of McGee's playboy reputation. What kind of a man made millions and used his working staff as his concubines? The more he heard of Rupert McGee the less he liked him.

"Do you know the McGee daughters?" Rollison asked, casually.

"Strewth, *no*! You see, they don't come to the East End."

"Mrs. McGee?" asked Rollison.

There was silence; and in it Rollison was able to manoeuvre the car into the highway he wanted and for the first time, swing into moving traffic at a fair pace. Preoccupied, minutes passed, before Edie spoke in a very gentle voice, almost as if a kind of lullaby.

"Poor old Alicia McGee. Poor old Alicia."

Rollison wasn't sure that he had heard aright but he did not want to ask; this girl responded best to silent prompting than to direct questions. They were in Commercial Road, surrounded by diesel fumes and petrol fumes and the crash and clank of engines and the ceaseless chatter of pistons, before Edie spoke again.

"She's a plaster saint," she declared.

"What kind of a saint?" he asked.

"She's just a saint. She takes what he hands out, and she—*do you know what?"* The question came out at the top of her voice, and suddenly she was clenching her fists and turning round and glaring at him. *"Do you know what?* She's always in and out of the factory. *She* looks after us! *She* does. *She* makes sure he doesn't drop us cold. She's always in the Welfare Department, everybody loves her. Oh, some laugh at her and some say she's a kind of harem mistress, but everybody loves her. All the women do, anyhow. And she knows everyone *and* everything that goes on."

Rollison thought: Does she, then?

Edie stopped; and drew in a deep breath; and looked away again. Rollison turned right, passed the Blue Dog two corners along, its windows bright, the Blue Dog on a sign vivid in a single floodlight. Next moment they were in Tenby Street, and Rollison was slowing down. "I can tell you this," the girl went on. "She was behind the shareholding lark—"

"The what?" asked Rollison puzzled.

"The shareholding lark. Every worker has some shares in the business, on top of wages—why, I've got a hundred myself. It's a kind of profit-sharing, and does it pay!"

"She sounds a remarkable woman," Rollison said, wondering very much about Alicia McGee. "What's the number of your house?"

"Seventy-one," Edie answered. "I-I just want to say—"

"You don't have to say a word," he assured her.

"I want to say you're a bloody good sort and I shouldn't have bored you like this."

"I'm not even slightly bored," Rollison said, and pulled up outside Number 71, a tiny house in a long terrace with the front door opening onto a narrow pavement. The street-lamps here seemed very far apart, and also dim. "Edie—what's your full name?"

"Edith White," she answered.

"Edie, I took a wrong turning in one way but I was at the factory because I was interested in it. Did you know that one of the McGee triplets has been kidnapped?"

"*No!*" she gasped.

"She has been. And I'm trying to find her."

"You're a *detective?*"

"In a way. How many people at the factory might hate the McGees enough to want to do them harm?"

Edie turned again to face him; this time, she took his hands. Her eyes were glistening brightly and the tension in her grip was great indeed.

"It's hard to say," she said. "Some hate them and some love them—especially Rupert. You see, a long time ago he gave shares in the business to all the workers, and there's this profit-sharing scheme. That and the big money is the main reason why a lot of people are for him. There's no doubt he's been a wonderful employer."

"I don't mean how many people think he's a good or a bad employer," Rollison said. "I mean how many people hate him personally—enough to want to do him harm."

Again, she paused, and her lips were working; when

the words came it was almost as if they burst from her lips.

"Hundreds!" she cried. "Hundreds!" She still held his hands, as if she would never let go, but very slowly her tension and her grip slackened, the brightness faded from her eyes, and she went on : "It's true, it's really true, but hundreds like him, too. My Pa, who's on the night shift, doesn't have any time for him. I—I *love* him!"

And she turned and opened the door, scrambling out as if she were afraid that he would call her back and ask her what she meant. She nearly ran into a cyclist, who swerved widely so as to dodge her, ran round the front of the car to the little house. The door opened as if by magic, a small child as well as Edie was outlined against bright light. Then the door closed and near blackness descended, and Rollison started off slowly, towards the Blue Dog.

"Mr. R," said Bill Ebbutt, "that's the way it is at McGees. If I'd known what you was after I could have told you all that girl did, and plenty more. I know dozens of people who work there. Come into the pub any night and you'll find two or three, at weekends you might find twenty. And what that girl told you is right on the nail. Those McGees really get people worked up one way and another. If working conditions weren't so good they'd never keep their staff." Ebbutt paused, then raised an admonishing finger. "And that's why I've got to say something to you. The McGees, mother, father and kids, aren't worth a patch on Jolly's trousers. Not even Alicia the Angel—Alicia the Devil she is, sometimes. Any woman who will let her husband carry on the way Rupert McGee does—well, she don't amount to much in my book. If you have to choose, make it Jolly. Don't take any risks with him."

"Have you been talking to Benbow?" asked Rollison.

"I've been talking with a lot of people, including

Benbow," answered Ebbutt earnestly. "Mr. R, forgive me being blunt, but you've always had an eye for a pretty face and those McGee kids are certainly easy on the eye. But if they disappeared and never turned up again, no one would miss them much, apart from the McGees. But Jolly—he's a different cup of tea. You'll give him absolute priority, Mr. R, won't you?"

CHAPTER XIII

Mystery Number

Rollison looked into Ebbutt's watery eyes, seeing the intensity in the flabby face, noticing that the full lips almost quivered, he was so anxious to make himself clear yet found it difficult to speak like this to the Toff. The first and vital thing was to reassure him; the second, although perhaps not yet, was to find out why he thought there might be the slightest fear of divided loyalty in his mind.

"Absolute priority, Bill," Rollison promised.

And Ebbutt demanded: "You're *sure*?"

Rollison stood in the room behind the bar of the Blue Dog, with the door closed and the noises muted. The pub was not so full as at lunchtime, but someone was shrieking as if hopelessly drunk. Ebbutt looked positively huge, small head, huge jowl, big sloping shoulders and vast chest making him look rather like an upturned pear. Rollison knew that he must find out what was going on in Ebbutt's mind.

"What makes you think I might not give Jolly priority, Bill?"

"*You* do, Mr. R." said Ebbutt, flatly.

"How?" asked Rollison, quite shaken.

"I know you," declared Ebbutt. "We all know you, Mr. R. You've taken some wild chances in your life, risked your life *and* risked Jolly's, because you've thought it's right. And once you start a job, you finish it. You don't care what the risks, you finish it. And if it happens to be for a pretty face, then, like I told you, you always seem to give it just that little extra. And now—" Ebbutt hesitated, at last at a loss for words, while Rollison, feeling cold inside, nevertheless smiled as brightly and spoke as gaily as he could.

"And now there are three pretty faces. Is that it?"

"And each one of them a real beauty," said Ebbutt.

"Tell me one thing, Bill," Rollison begged.

"Just ask," urged Ebbutt.

"What do you think I could have but haven't done, to help Jolly?"

Ebbutt pursed his lips and then exuded a long, wheezy breath.

"Well," he said, half-accusingly, "You've spent a lot of time with the McGee girls."

"When I could have been out looking for Jolly. Calling him, perhaps: Jolly, Jolly, Jolly, good boy, come to Rolly. Good God, Bill, what's got into you? What makes you think I haven't used every minute I could in what seemed to me the best way possible?"

It was a long time since he had felt the slightest lack of trust in Ebbutt. At the barge, he had understood Benbow's 'make it Jolly' as an indication of the man's concern for Jolly. He had not seen it as any kind of criticism. Now it began to look as if not only Benbow but Ebbutt and others whom Ebbutt had called on to help were accusing him of having more concern for the girls than for Jolly, who was like a part of himself.

It was a ludicrous idea.

"Mr. Rollison," said Ebbutt, "we aren't going to get anywhere by losing our tempers, are we?"

It was years, many years, since Ebbutt had used that formal 'Mr. Rollison', and that by itself was enough to pull Rollison up sharply. He felt a moment of shock, as if his mind had suddenly stopped working. Then it began to work at furious speed, while Ebbutt stood watching, defiantly, and the noises came from the bars. It was completely out of character for Ebbutt to react in such a way.

He hadn't, earlier in the day. Something he had learned or been told since then had changed his mood. There was a kind of coolness; suspicion of his, Rollison's, motives. And the rebuke "we aren't going to get anywhere by losing our tempers" was obviously meant to force the issue. He, Rollison, had to decide what to do. He hadn't much time even with his thoughts flashing fast, as they were; in this case he was always fighting against time. He could point out that he hadn't heard of the McGees until a few hours before, that every thinking moment since had been directly or indirectly for Jolly, that his promise of help for the triplets was simply to clear the way for helping Jolly. But these were the kind of arguments that would get nowhere at a time like this.

At last, he said: "Getting angry and showing it when you're being let down, is a lot better than going off sulking."

"*I* haven't let you down!"

"I think you have," Rollison said. "And if I let myself go I could knock your block off. I thought I knew you, thought I could trust you, but some sneaking liar whispers into your ear and you believe him. Who was it? Who's been getting at you?" When Ebbutt didn't answer at once but began to turn pink, Rollison went on roughly: "Come on, let's have the truth. Who have you been listening to?"

Ebbutt was now a bright pink, and his eyes were glittering.

"Why, you—" he began.

"Lets's have it," rasped Rollison. "First they get at Grice, who obviously thinks I'm involved, and then they get at you. The pair of you make me sick!"

"I've never been spoken to like this in my life!" Ebbutt wheezed.

"You've never asked for it from me before," Rollison said, calmly but very coldly. "Come on, Bill—who's been getting at you? And at Benbow. And at Grice? Who is trying to make sure I can't help the McGee girls? Who knows me enough to think that by kidnapping Jolly they can make me back down?" When Ebbutt didn't speak, but seemed to swallow incipient words, he went on: "Who's working on you? Tell me, and I'll go and work on him until he wishes he were dead—and I'll stop only when he's led me to Jolly."

When Rollison stopped, silence fell.

There was no way of being sure how Ebbutt would react; he might be bitterly and angrily resentful. He had turned turkey-red, as if the effect of keeping his self-control was almost too much for him. He might be weighing up the years of their friendship, looking at the situation through his, Rollison's, eyes. The certain thing was that he would soon know.

A buzzing sound came from the doorway, and Rollison knew almost as well as Ebbutt that this was an urgent summons for Ebbutt from one of the bars. Slowly, Ebbutt turned and flicked on a switch.

"What's up?" he demanded.

A Cockney voice sounded clearly about the room; there was a whispering, low, conspiratorial note about it.

"Bill," he said, "the cops is going to raid us."

"*What?*" breathed Ebbutt.

"There are four police cars, one at each corner, and two opposite the gym. The cops are getting out of their cars now. Some of the Divisional men is coming up too, so we've got the Flying Squad and the locals. No doubt about it, they're going to raid us."

"Okay," Ebbutt said. "Don't let anyone start anything."

"I won't, Bill."

"Anyone leaving?"

"Three or four walked out five minutes ago, they didn't want to be caught."

"Anyone know who the cops are after?" Ebbutt wanted to know.

"Not a whisper, Bill. *Bill!* I just 'ad a sign from Tommy, the cops are closing in!"

"Just make sure no one starts any trouble," Ebbutt urged, and flicked off the switch.

His colour had subsided and he looked much more himself, a powerful man of authority, very much master in his own domain: and this was his domain, with Rollison at best a visitor, almost an intruder. It was almost possible to see the thoughts flitting across Ebbutt's mind.

He said: "*You* know who they're after, don't you?"

"They're after me," Rollison said simply.

"And if I hide you and they find out, they could stop me running the Blue Dog, couldn't they?"

After a few seconds that seemed an age, Rollison said: "Yes, they could. And we can't risk that, can we?" he added under his breath. "Not even for Jolly's sake."

On the last words he moved away from Ebbutt to the door, so swiftly that the publican barely had time to call out. He opened the door, and the noise of talk and laughter took on almost a raucous note; news of the impending raid had spread, everyone who had stayed behind was making a little extra effort to appear happy and carefree. There was a sudden hush as Rollison appeared in the smoke-filled, over-heated room, an expectancy which he could not fail to notice.

As he stepped into full view there was a swift metamorphosis.

His expression and his manner changed; he was smiling and confident, there was a rollicking air about him, as if he had just come from a session which filled him with good humour. He threw: "I'll see you," over his shoulder, for Ebbutt might have followed, and raised his hands to the crowd in the saloon bar. A few murmurs of greeting came, a couple of men cocked thumbs, a little man called:

"How are yer, me old Toff?"

Rollison reached the door and pushed it open. The cold struck, knife-like, and made him wince. The street-lamps were misted over. Frost rimed the kerbs and even the surface of the pavement. Two men were coming towards

the Blue Dog from the right and the left, and he was walking towards those on the left. He saw them stiffen as they
recognised him. He made no attempt to evade them, and
became aware, from the sound of footsteps, that more men
had turned into the street from behind him; two more
were on the other side of the road. At least eight men were
close by.

The two on his side of the street stood still as he
approached them. Obviously, they expected him to run or
try to evade them; they seemed to stand at attention. But
he slowed down, somehow contrived to stop shivering, and
said:

"Hallo."

"Are you Mr. Rollison?" one man asked.

"Yes," said the Toff.

"We are police officers," the other man stated.

"Really," said Rollison as if greatly intrigued. "I don't
think we've met."

"No, sir. We must ask you—" the first man began.

"We would like you—" began the other.

"To come with you to the Yard," Rollison said. "Of
course. I'll be warm there, won't I?" he added brightly.
He placed his wrists close together, and proffered them.
"Do we clap on the darbies?"

"No need for that, sir," said the man who had spoken
first.

The two from the other side of the road had moved
across, much more relaxed. Those close behind also seemed
to relax, but Rollison himself was far, far from relaxation.
He had to make up his mind whether to make a break.
If he did, and was caught, it would only do harm. If he
did, and escaped, he would be on the run from the police
until this affair was over.

If Grice preferred a charge against him, would he be
able to get bail?

Why should Grice prefer a charge?

Why had Ebbutt behaved in such a way?

How could he find out if he were not free? How could he stay both free and active without help from Ebbutt?

A police car turned the corner, obviously the one he was to be taken away in. The dipped headlights seemed very bright on the frosted air; the stars were so bright and the night so peaceful.

In the gentlest of voices Rollison said: "Oh dear, I've forgotten my cigarette case."

He half-turned, and caught a glimpse of the men behind him; there *were* eight policemen in all. He spun back, placed a flattened hand against the chest of each of the two nearer policemen and thrust hard enough to send them staggering. The men behind shouted. The driver, face set, became a human gargoyle. Rollison ran at furious speed towards the end of the street, round it, then into the next—Tenby Street. The die was cast now; he had to get clear or be in deeper trouble. There were lights at windows, lights at fanlights, and there was still a light at Number 71. He reached it ahead of the police, pushed open the letter box and, as he had prayed, found the key dangling on a piece of string. He pulled this out, unlocked the door and stepped inside. Noises from a television set going full blast, beat at his ears. He closed the door, and leaned against it. A child laughed on a note of sheer delight. He heard footsteps outside, of running men. He heard one man speaking but could not catch the words. The clatter of footsteps passed, the noise of the television appeared to grow louder. It was surprisingly warm in here; too warm.

He couldn't stay; yet he couldn't go out like this.

He opened the door a fraction and again the cold cut into him. No one was in sight. He pressed the doorbell and then nipped back into the hall. A door at the end of the narrow passage opened, and Edie appeared, hot pants so short, hair so long.

She caught her breath in fright.

"It's all right," Rollison tried to reassure her. "It's all

right."

"*You!*" she breathed, and caught her breath. "You *are* the Toff, aren't you?"

"Yes, I—"

"I didn't realise until you'd gone! What—" She broke off, and then gasped: "What's the matter?"

"Did you say your father worked on the night shift at McGee's?"

"Yes," she breathed.

"Does he have an old suit of clothes I could borrow? And a cap?"

She stared at him with increasing alarm, she actually began to breathe faster. For a moment he thought she would begin to splutter out questions, out of a form of shock, but suddenly she moved towards the narrow stairs.

"I daresay," she said.

"Will they fit me?"

"They'd be a bit big."

"That won't matter," Rollison said.

She turned into a room at the head of the stairs, a tiny room which was in darkness. She flicked a switch and a dim light glowed from the ceiling. There was a double bed, a white wood wardrobe, a chair at one side of the bed. Over the tiny mantelpiece was a picture of Christ with some disciples. Edie pulled open the wardrobe door, and pulled out trousers, a jacket, a scarf and a cap, tossing them on the bed.

"Try 'em on," she urged.

The Toff slid out of his own jacket and trousers, and she stood holding out her father's pants. He took them and drew them on. They were big but not impossibly so, and there were braces which would hold them up. She was holding out the jacket but suddenly snatched it back.

"Half a mo'," she said, and rummaged, and then tossed a heavy tweed waistcoat towards him. "It's cold enough for that."

"Bless you! Will you take the things out of my pockets?"

She did so as he slid first into the waistcoat, then into the jacket; they felt both thick and warm. As she tossed his wallet, loose change, keys, cigarette lighter, matches and oddments onto the bed he picked them up and put them into the other pockets. The whole quick change took no more than three or four minutes, and Edie had not asked a single question.

"Get rid of my clothes, will you," he asked. "No, bundle them up, and —"

"The cops after you?" she demanded.

"Yes. There's been a little misunderstanding."

"They always know what they're doing," she said, with the now familiar bitterness. "I'll fix the clothes, Toff. Okay if they go to a jumble sale?"

"Couldn't be better," he approved.

"What about the cap?" she asked, handing it to him.

He put it on, and peered at himself in the little mirror. He caught a glimpse of Edie's reflection, too. She was smiling crookedly, quite attractively, as if getting a kick out of this.

"You look as if the cops *ought* to be after you," she observed.

"Edie, if they find out that you've helped me—"

"They'll be after me, too, I know. It's okay, Toff, no one will know. There's a clothes box at the church hall round the corner, I can dump these in on me way to the Blue Dog for a bit of company. What's up?" she asked, and it was the first time she had allowed her curiosity to show.

"When it's all over," Rollison said, "I'll come back and tell you. Thank you, Edie." As she came round the foot of the bed he gave her a quick, impersonal hug. "I'll never be able to thank you enough."

He went ahead of her down the narrow stairs. The television set was still blaring forth. He opened the street door as she suddenly moved forward and kissed him on the cheek, whispering:

"Good luck, Toff."

Then he stepped out into the street; and as the door closed behind him, a police car turned the corner on his right.

CHAPTER XIV

Toff Alone

Awareness that if he showed the slightest sign of the jitters the police would stop him, made Rollison turn right and walk briskly towards the corner. A glow in the sky not far away was from the Blue Dog and the gymnasium. Another door opened, light streamed out, and a man turned right, making Rollison miss a step. The police car, coming slowly, seemed about to stop. Rollison's heart beat like a trip hammer.

The car did stop, and the driver leaned out.

"Either of you seen a man running along here?"

The man in front of Rollison said: "Must be so thirsty he can't wait to get to the Blue Dog!"

"This isn't funny."

"Show me a cop who can see a joke," the other said. "You want a straight answer? I haven't seen anyone running tonight." He thrust his hands deeper into his pockets and stamped on, iron-tips on toes and heels making a kind of tap-dance.

Rollison hovered.

"I never see no one," he said. He might have been Ebbutt's man, with a Cockney voice so exaggerated that it had to be real. "Which way was 'e going?"

"Away from the Blue Dog."

"I never see no one," Rollison repeated.

The man next to the driver said something like: "We'll never catch him now." The driver grunted and started the car moving again. Rollison, looking down at his feet for fear of showing too much interest in the police car, passed beneath a street lamp and then had a shock which started his heart hammering again. His shoes were so highly polished they could give him away, no man dressed as he was would take such pains over his shoes. The car turned another corner. Rollison stepped into the kerb, where there was dry dirt and rubbish, bent down and picked up a handful, and rubbed it over his shoes. Now he felt safe; only a man looking him full in the face could suspect who he was. He did not turn towards the Blue Dog but to Commercial Road, where the lights were brighter and there was much more traffic and many more people about. He reached it as a little group came out of a pub, laughing and swearing among themselves. A policeman passed, looking at the group and not at the Toff. A few yards along there was a Number 15 bus, at a stop. He sprinted and caught it as the driver started off. The Negro conductress asked:

"Where to?"

He didn't want to go far.

"Aldgate East," he said.

"Two and a half pence," she replied, and punched and turned her ticket machine as he groped among bronze coins. She took the money and nodded, and he climbed the narrow, metalled stairs to the upper deck where only two couples sat, right at the back; each pair was absorbed in each other. He went near the front, looking down at the people and the cars and the few open shops and the dozens of closed ones—and it really dawned on him for the first time that he was alone; absolutely alone.

But he had learned a great deal.

There could be no doubt that someone whom both Grice and Ebbutt trusted, or some piece of evidence which seemed to be incontrovertible, had influenced each man. Ebbutt had been so absolutely convinced that he would put the McGee girls before Jolly that it made no sense.

Who, or what, could have caused this attitude?

As the bus paused at the traffic roundabout near Aldgate, he got up and walked along the narrow passage. One couple, looking dazed, were moving, obviously ready to get off. The other two still cuddled. He went down the twisting staircase.

Who, or what, could it have been?

He got off the bus into a crowded, brightly-lit scene, fruit barrow-boys were busy and noisy, cafés were open. A man in a bowler hat and dark coat was coming out of a café, and for a wild moment Rollison thought it was Jolly. But this man was both bigger and younger.

Where *was* Jolly?

He *must* go to the apartment in Giss Street and find out what he could of the couple in Apartment 4C. His visit there, the 'kidnapping' of the kidnapped Mary seemed long ago, in the age before Jolly had disappeared. The man had talked about her being worth a hundred thousand, and Rollison had thought it a simple case of kidnapping for ransom. Simple! The second place to go was the home of the McGees, Rupert McGee and his wife, Alicia the Angel—or Devil, as Ebbutt had said. She was one of the major mysteries, and he had to find out what she knew.

He crossed at a Zebra crossing to Aldgate East Station, went into a telephone box, and dialled his own number. It had hardly started ringing when Rose Sapelli answered, almost breathlessly.

"Who's that?"

"Hallo, Rose," said Rollison.

"Oh, thank God you've rung!" breathed Rose. "I thought you were never going to! The cops only went an hour ago, I thought they was never going, and they're watching the flat back and front. Whatever you do don't come back—that's if you don't want to be picked up. *Have you found Jolly?*" The words of the question came like a succession of bullet shots.

"Not yet," Rollison said. "Do you know what they want me for?"

"You mean *you* don't?"

"No."

"For *murder*, Mr. R."

Rollison thought : It can't be. And then he wondered; who has been murdered? Next he thought, sickeningly, that it could be Jolly—but no! That was nonsense, or Rose wouldn't have asked if he'd found Jolly.

Then who?

Marie McGee . . .?

"Whose murder?" he demanded.

"A man and a woman at Giss Street, Fulham."

His heart went heavy and cold within him. Who else could the couple be but the man and woman who had kidnapped Mary McGee? He hadn't known their name, but there could hardly be any doubt; so he was too late to find out anything from them. He was silent for a long time, and regretted among other things that Grice must have deliberately allowed Rose to know all this so that she could pass it on. At last he forced himself to ask :

"Did Grice say anything else, Rose?"

"All he wanted to know was where you'd been last night, and as I didn't know I couldn't tell him, could I? He sent men to see Bill Ebbutt, and sent others to your aunt, what's her name—"

"Old Glory?" ejaculated Rollison.

"It sounded like first or burst."

"*Hirst.*"

"That's it! I can tell you one thing, Mr. R. You left some fingerprints."

"Where?"

"At the scene of the murder, of course, where else would they matter?"

"I couldn't leave fingerprints at a place I haven't been," Rollison said, sharply. He must never admit that he had been there; not to Rose, nor to anyone.

"You haven't been?" echoed Rose. "You mean you didn't do it?"

"Don't be silly, Rose. Of course I didn't."

"Bless me for a lemon," she exclaimed. "I must say I thought—" She broke off. "Well, I can tell you that Gricey and his men think you did it. They think you lost your self-control because you were so mad about Jolly—and then—" She broke off, with a catch in her breath, and Rollison didn't know whether it was from fright or because she changed her mind about what to say. He could hear her breathing, so she was holding the mouthpiece very close. Then she spoke again in an urgent whisper: "The cops are back. They took a key."

"What were you going to say?" asked Rollison, almost desperately. Then the pips began to sound, his time had run out; but he had two more twopenny pieces and rammed them in the slot.

"I forget, the cops—oh, I remember," Rose was saying. "And then they thought you were going to do a deal with the McGee girls, to get Jolly. They know he's missing, Bill Ebbutt told them. Mind you, I only heard bits and pieces of what they said, Mr. Rollison. They—"

A man called loudly: "Is that Rollison?" There was a thudding sound and before Rollison could put down the receiver, a man seemed to bellow in his ear. "You haven't a chance! If you don't give yourself up every newspaper in the country will publish your photograph under a 'Wanted For Murder' headline."

Rollison's voice was very steady.

"And if I give myself up, the only change will be 'Arrested' for 'Wanted'. Give Mr. Grice a message for me, will you?"

"If you don't give—"

"Tell him I didn't do it." Rollison talked over the man's voice. "And tell him there is only one thing that would make me give myself up."

In a quieter yet eager voice, the detective said: "What's that?"

"If I were sure it was the only way I could find Jolly," Rollison said, and rang off.

For the few minutes while he had been talking to Rose, he had been oblivious of traffic; for a few moments longer, he still was. Then he heard a tapping, and saw a long-haired youth at the kiosk door, tapping with a coin. Rollison pushed open the heavy door, and the youth grunted:

"What's the matter? Having a nap?"

"I'm sorry," Rollison said, in his normal speaking voice, and the youth looked back at him in surprise. Someone came out of the next kiosk and he went in and checked the McGees' address in the directory. Rupert McGee, 1 Mansell Square, was the address he was after. He fumbled for more coins and had only one twopence; so this call shouldn't last long. He dialled the Mayfair number, wanting only to find out whether Mrs. McGee was in. After a moment or two, a woman answered.

"This is Mayfair 23412." The voice was soft and pleasing.

"Is Mrs. McGee in, please?"

"This is she speaking."

"Mrs. McGee," Rollison said quietly, "this is Richard Rollison. I don't know whether your daughters have mentioned me."

"Yes indeed they have," answered Mrs. McGee with gentle emphasis. "Mary in particular has been most enthusiastic. How very nice of you to call. Do you want to speak to one of my daughters? I'm afraid—"

"I wanted to know whether you had heard from them this evening," Rollison interrupted.

"No, I haven't," answered Mrs. McGee, regretfully. "They have their own apartments, of course, and I often don't see them during the day. Is there any message I can give them?" There was a hint of a chuckle in her voice.

"You might tell them I called," Rollison said.

"I will do that," Mrs. McGee assured him. "They may telephone—one of them usually does."

"Thank you, Mrs. McGee." Rollison was brisk. "Good night."

"Good night to you," she said pleasantly, and her receiver went down.

Rollison replaced his very slowly and thoughtfully, looked round, made sure no one was watching, and saw the people going to and fro along the street and towards the stairs leading down to the trains. No one took any notice of him. He kept thinking of the pleasant voice and its note of unconcern. Her daughters led their own lives and this did not appear remotely to trouble her. No mother could talk with such casual charm, surely, if she had the faintest suspicion that one of her daughters had been kidnapped.

If he went to see her he might learn more.

Slowly, he lifted the receiver, and dialled 100. Almost at once the operator answered.

"Will you find out if the subscriber at Wimbledon 27175 will transfer the charges on this call?" asked Rollison. "He is a Mr. Grice—"

"One moment, sir. What is your number?"

Rollison read it out from the circular panel on the instrument.

Quiet fell; the near silence with muffled footsteps and whispering and echoing on the line. Grice would take the call, but he might be quick-witted enough to try to check the number of the call-box, and he could have police here in a few minutes. This would show whether, at home, he was prepared to listen, or whether he would be as coldly hostile as when others had been within earshot.

Suddenly, the operator said: "You're through."

"Hallo, Bill," Rollison said mildly.

"Rolly!" exclaimed Grice.

"That's much better," Rollison said with relief; and he added promptly : "I didn't do it."

"So your new maid said," Grice responded drily. "Where are you?"

"At a call-box in Aldgate."

"I suppose you know that nothing I do can help now," Grice said, grimly.

"Bill, I know nothing about the murder of the people in Giss Street," Rollison declared with great precision.

"But you were there," Grice said. "Your fingerprints are quite beyond doubt."

There was no use in arguing now; or making a denial. Grice would know they were his fingerprints, and denial would simply prove that he was lying. So he said :

"Before they were killed, Bill."

"The only way you can help yourself now is to give yourself up, and tell us exactly what happened. Then we can check your story against the established facts, and—"

"I'll give myself up the moment I find Jolly," Rollison promised.

Silence fell.

Something about the way it dropped, at the moment when he had expected a quick retort, disturbed him. As the silence lengthened he felt almost like shouting : "What are you holding back?" Could they be cut off? No : he heard a muted cough, and wondered whether Grice's wife, or someone with him at the flat, was on another telephone.

At last Grice said with great precision : "Jolly's clothes were found by a police officer near the river at Chelsea."

"*Clothes?*" echoed Rollison, tensely.

"Everything he would wear."

"You mean you think he threw himself in the river?" asked Rollison incredulously.

"I think someone has tried to make it look as if he committed suicide," stated Grice, flatly.

"That way, on a night like *this!*"

"Rolly," Grice said, "I can only tell you what I know. All of Jolly's clothes were found by the river—on Chelsea Steps. The Thames Division is on the lookout for his body, of course. There's no certainty. If they had been your clothes I would have thought you were trying to pretend you'd jumped into the river, but why on earth should Jolly try to fool us?"

Hoarsely, Rollison said: "I can't imagine. And it doesn't make sense in any weather."

"The suicide evidence might have been left behind if in fact he was murdered," Grice reasoned. "Have you the faintest idea where he went last night?"

"No," Rollison said. "Not the faintest."

He rang off, and went out immediately but no one appeared to be taking any notice of him, Grice hadn't apparently moved fast. Just at that moment, as the icy wind sliced at him, Rollison felt as cold in heart as he did in body.

CHAPTER XV

Angel

Rollison needed not only time to think, but time to recover before he could go to the house in Mansell Square. He went into a steak house near Aldgate East Station and ordered a steak and chips, biscuits and cheese and hot coffee. It was the first reasonable meal he had had for an age. Finished, he caught a bus from across the road, to Knightsbridge. The bus was crowded with people from the pubs and the cinemas, all of which were closing. He got off opposite Harrods. Theatre traffic was heading *en masse* towards the suburbs, but few people walked in the streets, and those few were huddled up against the cold. He tightened the muffler about his neck and walked very fast across the road towards the network of streets and squares between here and Kensington Gore. He knew Mansell Square; in his youth he had often been taken to visit an uncle who lived there.

Often, by Jolly!

He felt as if he were in a fog. There seemed no sense in what had happened, no reason at all why it should have begun. First, the McGee girls had set out to involve him, and how hard they had worked! Next the man with the slightly accented voice had called him on the telephone.

Why had it been so important—first, that he should help the triplets, second, that he should not? He had not the slightest idea what the answers were. He turned a corner into Mansell Square, and a savage gust of wind made him shiver through and through; these heavy clothes and the thick muffler might almost have been made of cotton. He slipped into the big porch, picturing a naked body in the near-freezing river.

Such a fate couldn't have overcome Jolly.

But . . . it was just possible.

No light showed at the fan-shaped light above the doorway; and there had been none at any of the windows. A house like this might be chained and bolted, there was no way of telling until he tried the lock. He used a skeleton key but his hands soon got so cold that he dropped the key twice. He needed Mick Carter here, Mick could have been on the other side of the door in a couple of jiffs. But he couldn't call on Mick now; couldn't rely on any of Ebbutt's contact men.

What had changed Ebbutt?

At last, the lock clicked back; he turned the handle and pushed. The door yielded an inch, but didn't open. He thought : It's chained, and was taken by another fit of shivering. When this passed he tried again, and the door opened so suddenly that he nearly fell inside. For a sudden, panic-stricken moment he thought that someone had pulled it open, but no : it had been jammed, and given way under pressure.

He stepped inside and began to close the door. Wind snatched it out of his hand, slamming it. He found himself in a small lobby, a kind of airlock. Beyond was another closed door. He stood in a corner, pressing tightly against it, fearful that the slamming had been heard.

Nothing stirred; perhaps this was a sound as well as an air trap.

He turned the handle of the second door, which was unlocked, pushed warily, heard nothing, and stepped inside. A faint light shone at a half-landing, showing the spacious hall, the furniture, the pictures; he had a sense of luxury, of antiquity. There were rugs which he could hardly distinguish on the floor, and a circular staircase, like the one he had walked up as a boy.

Walked up—and slid down.

"It is not so much that you might break your neck," Jolly would say, "rather that you might find your uncle disapproves, and in disapproving, punish you by reducing the size of the gift he ordinarily gives."

Rollison could almost hear Jolly's voice; almost see the man who had been so much younger then and yet in so many ways was just the same now. He walked to the stairs. They weren't really in the position, he recalled, the old house was in the opposite corner of the square; but the similarity was almost uncanny. He ran his hand over the curve of the banister; the wood was cold but the house struck warm after the streets and squares.

It was too big a house to check every room, so he really had little doubt what to do first : begin by finding Alicia McGee.

She wouldn't sleep on the ground floor.

He went up the lovely staircase, keeping to one side lest it should creak, but it was a solid one; as solid as the house's foundation. On a half-landing a dim light burned. He heard no sound. As he reached the next main landing, he paused. There was no burglar alarm, as far as he had seen; no dog; nothing to protect the house against burglars. That seemed absurd.

Could it be a trap, to lure him so far into the house that he couldn't escape?

Why him? How could anyone know that he would come here?

It could be a trap for someone else—

Or it could simply be that the doors had not been locked and the alarm system not switched on. It was still early, half-an-hour or so before midnight. Members of the household, family or staff, might still be out. The house seemed shut up for the night, but—

He heard a noise below, turned, and looked over the

landing. The front door was opening. A woman appeared, followed by a man. The man looked up at the wall by the side of the door, reading something Rollison hadn't noticed. He said in a clear voice :

"Jackson isn't in yet."

"She stays out *much* too late," declared the woman.

"She has permission until one-thirty," the man replied in a flat voice.

"You shouldn't have to stay up every night to see her in."

"Oh, be quiet, Helen," the man said impatiently.

They walked to the side of the stairs, their footsteps now hard on wooden flooring, now muffled by rugs. They disappeared, obviously to the domestic quarters. Unless these had been remodelled or were different from the house he remembered, he could have gone from pantry to kitchen, larder to cold room, cold room to scullery, scullery to the small, walled garden which had no doorway except from the house.

Rollison's main question was answered.

He turned from the top of the stairs towards the main landing, then saw a crack of light close to the ground. He stood watching, gradually able to make out a straight line, as at the foot of a door, but no door outline. Stepping forward, he discovered why; there was a heavy drape at the door, either to keep out draught or to keep out noise. He stretched up and groped. The curtain hung from big rings on a pole, secured on the left. He eased the rings gently over the pole until the shape of a door was outlined by light. This was a small suite of rooms— God, how well he remembered! His uncle and aunt could shut themselves off from the rest of the household. They hadn't had a curtain but a double door, and when both were closed, no one had been allowed to enter.

He listened intently, and thought he heard voices. He groped again, found the handle and turned.

It wasn't locked.

He pushed the door open wider, with memory flooding back. A passage beyond served bedroom, dressing room, living room and bathroom. A light shone from the ceiling onto the four closed doors. The voices sounded louder against a background of music. He turned, to find the key in the lock of the door by which he had entered. He turned it, startled by the loudness of the click, undecided whether to leave it in the keyhole or put it in his pocket; he left it, and turned back.

At the right end of the passage was the bathroom, very contemporary and with a sunken bath shaped like an oyster shell. A dim light was on; why were the lights so dim everywhere? The room at the other end was the main bedroom, also with a diffused light; there were two-double-sized beds in a huge room. He entered this and crossed to a door which stood ajar: this led into the dressing room.

Voices came much more clearly; so did the music. He could not distinguish the words but a man was doing most of the talking. As Rollison drew nearer the door leading to the sitting room, he heard him say:

"At least we are agreed about that, 'Licia, so we don't need to discuss it."

· Rollison caught his breath. For this was the voice of the man who had telephoned the warning not to help the McGee girls!

"I have to be sure you understand," the woman said, as the realisation flashed into Rollison's mind.

The man laughed.

"I understand, my darling!"

"I hope you do," she said. "It would be very expensive if you didn't."

"You worry too much about money," the man replied.

"Make sure you worry enough," she retorted. For a few moments only the music came, and Rollison placed his fingers on the door handle. If he made a sound it would be heard, but he could cope from here on. He turned the handle a fraction as the man said :

"How long will Rupert be away?"

"Long enough," the woman answered.

"You must be more explicit, 'Licia! I can't work in the dark all the time."

"Sometimes," she said, "you will have to."

Rollison now pushed the door open a crack. There was no sound from it, but suddenly the music seemed louder, and he thought he could detect the heavy breathing of man or woman. The door opened an inch, and he could see a part of the room.

He could not have been better placed. A fire was blazing in a big hearth in the wall on the left. A woman's hand showed on the arm of a winged armchair and a man sat in a similar chair on the other side of the fire-place. His profile was turned towards Rollison. If he turned to look round he would see the open door; even while looking at the woman, he would probably become quickly aware of movement from the door. He had a good profile; prominent chin, rather hooked nose, high fore-head and well-marked eyebrows. He wore a silken dressing-gown, and what looked like pale-grey pyjamas. The fire-light flickered yellow and red on his face, giving him a positively Mephistophelian appearance, although he had so far been on the defensive.

He leaned forward, stretching out a hand; the woman's hand, scintillas of light coming from the rings on it, appeared for him to take it. He closed his other hand about it.

" 'Licia, my darling, don't you think you can trust me? You must know I have only your interest at heart."

She didn't draw her hand away as she said : "You are like all of us, Michael : you come first to yourself."

"Yes, of course," the man agreed, "but my best interests are served in serving you."

"A *very* pretty phrase," she half-derided.

"It's a simple truth," he insisted.

"You mean, if it would serve your interest best you would cheerfully cut my throat."

The phrase sounded ugly, coming from a woman who seemed to mean it literally. It made the man draw in a sharp breath and relax his hold. When the woman went on it was with a hint of a laugh in her voice.

"Well, wouldn't you, Michael?"

"You know perfectly well that I wouldn't."

"Not with a knife, but—"

"If you mean would I betray you to Rupert, I most certainly would not."

"Unless he offered you more money than you could hope to get from me, Michael dear." Now she leaned forward and for the first time Rollison was able to see her. She was striking-looking, with silver-grey hair. The most surprising thing was that she was nothing like her daughters; they were beautiful in a pretty way, she was strikingly beautiful with a hint of regality about her features. "Don't fool yourself or pretend to fool me," she went on. "We have been lovers because it has suited us, not because I have a passionate love for you, or you for me. And we are business partners because it suits us to be—and pays us to be. I don't want the bother of breaking in another lover and you have become so used to living here when Rupert is away and running both his and my affairs that you really don't want to change. If Rupert came and offered you a million pounds for the truth I've no doubt you would say no, but if it mattered enough for him to pay five million, I think you would accept."

When she broke off, Michael did not respond; nor did he draw his hands away. Rollison pushed the door open wider so that he could see further into the room and get inside with a single stride.

"You really must be the most cold-blooded woman alive," the man said, with a note of incredulity tinged perhaps with disgust. "Why, even while—"

"Michael, isn't it true?" she interrupted. "If Rupert

were to offer enough, wouldn't you betray me?"

After a long pause, he said: "Until tonight, nothing would have made me. After tonight—yes, I suppose I would."

"So it shouldn't surprise you if I keep you in the dark about some things," she said.

"I suppose not," the other conceded grudgingly.

"Then we really do understand each other about that. Tell me, did you kill the Elliots?"

"Alicia!"

"Well, did you?"

After another pause, the man named Michael said: "You can't be surprised if I keep some things to myself."

She laughed.

"Touché. But why did you?"

"If you read the newspapers tomorrow you will learn that a certain Mr. Toff Rollison killed them."

"Will you let him be found guilty for a crime you committed?" Alicia McGee asked. There was curiosity in her voice but no sense of shock or disgust as far as Rollison could tell.

"Of course," Michael answered.

"*Is* he so dangerous?" the woman wanted to know.

"If allowed to stay free he could be deadly." Michael had no doubt at all.

"Simply because the girls went to him for help?"

"Partly because of what they might tell him and partly because of what he might find out. 'Licia, we have too much at stake to allow some gallivanting romantic to interfere. I know too much about Rollison to have any doubt: he could ruin us. Do you know whom he took home tonight?"

"I can't wait to hear."

"Edie White," said Michael, softly.

"My goodness!" exclaimed Alicia McGee. "Edie? How on earth did he get on to her?"

"I'm not sure that he did. He was parked near the

factory and she stood and chatted him up, then went off
in his car," answered Michael. "He'll attract others, bees
to a honey-pot. It's almost as if that man has some sixth
sense when investigating crime."

"Oh, nonsense! He may have widespread sources of
information but don't talk to me about a sixth sense or
extrasensory perception," the woman retorted sharply.
"You do feel sure that the police will charge him with
the Elliots' murder?"

"I am positive."

"Who told you?"

"Young Adrian Bell," answered Michael, and Rollison
drew in a sharp and almost audible breath. "Superintendent Grice is an old friend of Rollison, and if he could
avoid it he would, but the fingerprints are there, Rollison
was seen to go in and seen to leave. His extrasensory
perception didn't tell him that I have the Elliots watched
day and night. He brought Mary away, and took her
to his flat. That was when I really had to move fast. I
assure you that no one else would have moved so fast or
so effectively! Of course, he was very lucky but he did
get to Globe Crescent very quickly and afterwards he
moved like lightning. I had to make sure he couldn't go
on, that is why I lured his man Jolly away, and made
sure Rollison was too distracted to concentrate on your
pretty daughters."

"But don't I understand that he concentrated well
enough to spirit two of them away?" asked Alicia McGee.
"So that we cannot play our usual tricks with them?"

That was the moment when she freed her hand from
Michael's.

And that was the moment when Rollison realised that
the mother of the triplets was aware of, and perhaps a
party to, the misadventures of Mary, Marie and Maria,
over the years.

CHAPTER XVI

Motive?

Rollison was so surprised that he tightened his grip on the handle of the door, and thrust it forward. But Michael Unknown, not looking his way, didn't notice the movement. He seemed as shocked, in a different way; certainly he didn't answer at once. The woman leaned forward, smiling a curiously dry smile. She was in control of the situation, playing with the man as if he were a musical instrument.

She was Alicia the Angel, remember!

She knew of, might well have been a party to, the kidnapping of her daughters.

Oh no, Rollison thought, that can't make sense.

Michael Unknown settled back in his chair and asked in a muted tone: "How on earth did you know that Rollison spirited them away? That *I* haven't got them?"

"I have to use my wits, Michael, and you are not yourself. This Toff has frightened you. You are even prepared to frame him for murder. What could he have done but take the girls so that you can't bargain with them?"

"You're an ogre," the man declared.

"You hoped to find them and get them back in time to prevent me from finding out," went on Mrs. McGee. "You should have known you haven't a chance, Michael. I have informants everywhere. What other reasons have you for blaming this Toff for the Elliots' murder? To save your own neck, or to keep Rollison out of the way?"

"Both," Michael said huskily.

"Do you know where he is now?"

"I—I *think* so."

"You think," the woman half-sneered. "Do you know?"

"I think he's hiding in an East End pub."

"The Blue Dog?"

"You—you're uncanny," muttered the man in a helpless way. "You really are. Yes, I think so."

"He left there over an hour and a half ago, and managed to outwit the police," Alicia McGee informed him. "They don't know where he is, and you most certainly don't. He may even be here." She said that in the silkiest of voices, as if she were deliberately tormenting the man.

"For God's sake! That's not funny."

"It wasn't meant to be funny. He telephoned me," she added.

That was the moment when the man turned round in his seat, and saw the Toff. The expression on his face froze so instantly that the woman also turned her head; and her face dropped. They sat absolutely motionless, staring.

Rollison stepped inside and closed the door.

He saw the man shift position and begin to lift his right hand, obviously towards a bell-push in the fire-surround. Rollison moved with calculated speed, reaching the chair as the man tried to spring up from it. Rollison put his weight on the back of the chair, and it toppled backwards, the man gasped and his arms and legs began to wave. Rollison thrust an extra leverage, and the chair went further back, carrying the man with it. On the instant, Rollison turned to the woman, who had gripped a handbag on her lap. He snatched the bag, opened it and turned it upside down. A pearl-handled pistol, some cigarettes, some bottles and some money fell out. He moved with that same devastating speed, held the woman round the shoulders with one arm and bent down and picked up the little gun.

The man had crashed down, his legs thrashing wildly as

he strove to get to his feet, but he was at Rollison's mercy.
There was a chance that the falling of the chair had been
heard and would bring someone up, but there were no
sounds.

Alicia McGee said, in a strangled voice : "You really
are the Toff, aren't you? What a remarkable man!"

"Not so remarkable as angry," Rollison said coldly.
"Don't rely on my so-called gallantry. I regard the sexes
as equal if they threaten trouble." He opened the handle
of the pistol, glanced down, said: "Thank you for loading
it. I shall shoot you if you interfere."

"I really believe you would," she said.

"You really believe right," Rollison assured her. "Now—
you." He pointed the gun towards Michael Unknown, who
was on one knee, and who should be on his feet in a few
seconds. "Where is Jolly?"

"I—I—how should I know?"

"For your sake, I hope you do," Rollison said roughly.
"If you don't I am going to break your neck."

"You—you must be mad! How on earth can I—"

Rollison said: "I've been here for twenty minutes, and
I've heard all you've said. I know that you killed or
arranged the killing of the Elliots. I know how clever you
think you are. Let us find out if you're clever enough to
save your own life. Where is Jolly?"

The woman had settled back in her chair, but otherwise
hadn't moved. Her eyes were shining, her face glistening,
as if this were a spectacle she revelled in. Her hands were
on the arms of the chair and she seemd to offer no threat.

This could well be the moment when she was at her
most dangerous.

The man Michael made another ineffective attempt to
get up, but dropped down again and was worse off than
before. There was the shadow of fear in his eyes.

"I don't think I've ever been in such a cold rage in my
life," Rollison said icily. "You have framed me for murder,
so choking the life out of you won't make much difference.

Where is Jolly?"

"Oh, my God!" Michael Unknown cried. "I tell you I don't know. If you were here when we started talking you ought to know. She spirited him away somewhere. I brought him here but she took him away. Don't ask me—ask her."

Rollison turned his head very slowly towards the woman, and saw that she was smiling.

It was no ordinary smile, but one of sheer enjoyment. Rollison had not the slightest doubt that she did know where Jolly was, and it would be much harder to make her talk than to make the man. This was the first time he had looked at her, full face. She *was* beautiful, but the beauty was marred—unless in fact it was accentuated—by the slightest of casts, so slight that at first he had to ask himself what it was.

"So you were right," he remarked drily.

"About what? I—oh. Yes." She looked at the helpless man. "About Michael letting me down under pressure. I really had no doubts about Michael. May he get up?"

"No. Who is he?"

"Michael? You mean you don't know?"

"There is a world outside the world of McGee's Soup," Rollison observed.

"Of course," she said, and added contritely: "I'm sorry. Michael Gogarty is the Public Relations Officer for McGee's Soup, Mr. Rollison. And in his way a very good one."

"I see that he carries on his public relations in private places," Rollison said, tartly. "How long have the pair of you been playing put-and-take with your lovely daughters?"

"What an apt way of describing it," applauded Alicia McGee. "Take them here, put them there." Rollison waited as she paused, and then went on: "For a very long time."

"From what Mary, or is it Maria, told me, since they

were babes-in-arms."

"Well, in prams, anyhow." Her eyes laughed.

"You must have caught Michael Gogarty very young," remarked Rollison.

"I was only twenty!" Gogarty burst out. "I didn't know what I was doing!"

"Really?" said Rollison, with deceptive gentleness. He saw the disgust in the woman's face as he went on: "But you knew what you were doing when you killed the Elliots, didn't you?" After a pause he went on: "Get up."

Gogarty, almost gasping for breath, at last managed to struggle to his feet. His hair hadn't been disturbed, he was still copy-book handsome but for the fear livid in his grey eyes and somehow heightened by his wet lips.

"Telephone Wimbledon 27175," Rollison ordered, and he raised the gun a little, menacingly. With trembling fingers Gogarty scrambled to the telephone on a table by Alicia's chair and began to dial.

"W-w-what number did you say?"

"Wimbledon 27175."

"Who—what is it?"

"Never mind."

After three false starts, Gogarty made the call. The ringing sound was so loud that it could be heard all over the room. Rollison moved closer to the telephone, near both man and woman now. The woman looked puzzled and wary.

At last a man replied : "Grice here."

"What—what—what do I have to say to him?" stammered Gogarty.

"Just tell him you murdered the Elliots," said Rollison very precisely. "Tell him you had seen me go into their flat earlier and after I'd left you went in and killed them."

"But I didn't!" Gogarty cried. "It was Kidd! He had a room opposite them, he was watching!"

Rollison remembered the man he had seen in Giss Street, bundled up against the cold. Had that been Kidd?

And he remembered the raid on his flat as he went on:

"Kidd was the man you sent to my flat, wasn't it? Why did you send him?"

Gogarty didn't answer. It was hard to understand a man collapsing so utterly; Gogarty seemed unable to speak. The silence, broken only by his heavy breathing, was answer enough, and Rollison went on coldly:

"Did Jimmy Tidy come to warn me what was going on? Is that what the shindig at my flat was about? Is that why he was killed? Come on! Answer me!"

"I didn't know Kidd was going to kill anyone!"

"You telephoned me and warned me not to help the McGee girls. *Why?* What little game are you up to?"

Two things happened at the same time. A glint shone in Gogarty's eyes, and he dropped the telephone receiver, then grabbed the whole instrument and hurled it at Rollison. As he ducked, Alicia McGee clawed at Rollison's right hand holding the gun. Her nails lacerated the flesh and he dropped the gun. He made a grab at it, missed his footing, and fell sideways on one leg; and the woman, suddenly on her feet, hooked his other leg from under him.

He had only a split second to think and act.

He felt the heat of the glowing fire as he stretched out a steadying hand towards it. For an awful moment he thought that his hand would plunge into the coals, he had completely lost his balance and there was no way of saving himself. He made a desperate effort, twisted his body round, touched the side of the fireplace, which was hot enough to sting, then felt himself grabbed by the left arm and pitched to one side, away from the fireplace. One moment he was plunging towards the burning coals, the next he was away from them, staggering, aware of nothing but relief. He thudded bodily into a wall, jolting himself from head to foot so badly that he nearly lost consciousness.

He slumped down, aware only of one thing: fear of what they would do. But he was beyond action, beyond positive thought, aware of pain in his back, pain at the side of his right hand, and near oblivion. His vision was blurred, there were peculiar noises in his head.

No one came to him; no one touched him.

Soon, he was able to straighten out; arms, back, legs. He was by the side of a table. He eased himself into the right position, then managed to get to his feet. The pain in his back was bad but not enough to prevent him from moving. Gradually his vision cleared, until he could see about the room.

It was empty.

The chair was still on its back, a small table, books, glasses and whisky on the floor lying near it. Whisky had spilled into a damp patch on the dark red carpet. The telephone was on the floor, platform in one place, receiver in the fireplace. Fire irons were scattered all over the white hearth.

On Alicia McGee's chair was an unbelievable sight: the pistol. He picked it up and checked the handle magazine. It was still loaded. Such a woman wouldn't overlook that, so she had left it deliberately. He slipped it into his pocket, and took some unsteady steps towards the door. He turned the handle and thrust; but the door was locked from the outside.

Every movement an effort, he turned towards the windows, where heavy tapestry curtains were drawn. He pulled one. Beyond were French windows leading to a balcony. He unlocked the door and stepped outside. In that moment he had forgotten the cold, and the shock was as bad as diving into an icy pool. He gritted his teeth and leaned against the balcony.

Beneath a street-lamp near-by stood a man and a girl, huddled together; necking at near zero! The man looked up, and light streamed from the front door of the house, quite brilliant.

The man with the girl was Adrian Bell!

If that wasn't shock enough, the man who stormed out

of the house—Gogarty—stopped for a split second in a headlong rush, and stared at both man and girl, as if in recognition. Then he rushed towards the corner, and Rollison had no doubt where he was heading; behind the square was a mews, his car would be parked there.

Rollison could call: "After him, Bell! There's your story!"

But young Bell would recognise his voice, would know that finding him, Rollison, was story enough. If Bell came up here it would spoil all chance of what Rollison wanted most: another talk with Alicia McGee, about Jolly; above all, about Jolly. He had a swift thought which stabbed him with fear: that she might have sent Gogarty to kill Jolly, but the thought was stillborn. Gogarty was on the run, soon this place would be surrounded and the police were bound to be after him; he would be concerned only with his own safety.

Suddenly, Adrian Bell said: "Who was that?"

"Oh, don't worry about him, that's Alicia's boyfriend! Adrian dear, I could easily smuggle you up to my room—"

Then the door opened again and a man called: "Jackson! Jackson!" That was the man who had come in when Rollison had just broken in. What sounded like: "I must fly," came from Adrian Bell, who broke away from the girl and went swiftly after Gogarty. The girl stood staring after him and more words floated up. *"You scared pig!"* The man appeared from the front door, saying: "Jackson, you'll catch your death of cold." He put his arm round her, and it did not seem wholly protective.

They disappeared; and the door closed, shutting off the light.

Adrian Bell disappeared round the corner.

Rollison drew back into the big room, and closed the French windows; it now seemed as cold in here as it had on the balcony. The room was still empty, the door was still locked.

Had Alicia McGee run away, too? he wondered.

And would Bell follow Gogarty far? Bell had denigrated his own physical courage, but Gogarty had much less. Yet Gogarty was frightened and at bay: he could be very dangerous, and young Bell could well be his next victim.

Adrian Bell turned into the mews as a car engine started up. An M.G. sports car was facing him, the lights on 'park'. Light spread from street-lamps, and he could see the driver clearly but took it for granted that he was Gogarty. The McGee story was building up into something really sensational and he, Bell, needed a new angle, preferably one that wouldn't involve the girls. So he went forward in front of the car, the thin-soled shoes he was wearing moulding painfully to the cobbles. While he was in front of the car there could be no danger. He actually called out:

"Mr. Gogarty. Spare me a—"

Before he said 'minute' the engine roared and the car moved forward in a racing start.

CHAPTER XVII

Near Misses

Adrian Bell knew exactly what was going to happen and he felt an awful fear. Instinctively he flung himself to one side. He felt the gust of wind as the car passed and pain stabbed through his ankle, but he wasn't badly hurt. He rolled over, gasping, and stared as the red light disappeared out of the mews, heading for Knightsbridge. Very slowly, he picked himself up. He winced when he put his right foot to the ground, and tested it gingerly; it wasn't too bad. He limped towards the mews exit, and looked right, in time to see the light disappearing again.

"Not a hope," he said *sotto voce*.

His own car was parked near the McGees' house, and he went slowly towards the corner of Mansell Square, debating with himself whether to phone in a story that he, a member of the reporting staff of the *Echo* had nearly been run down by the P.R.O. of McGee's Soups. He decided that he needed time to think. Perhaps the best thing would be to drive to Fleet Street and tell the Night Editor in person. He moved to his car and got in. The ankle was a little more painful but he could still move it.

He glanced up at the house as he drove past, but did not see Rollison, who had watched him get into the car and start off.

At least he's not hurt, Rollison said to himself as he turned back to the room, and thought of Adrian Bell

soon faded. It looked as if he had been 'on duty' with
the girl Jackson, probably insinuating himself into the
domestic side of the household. He, Rollison, had lost
Gogarty, and short of telling the police whom to look
for, there was nothing he could do. If he named Gogarty,
Grice would soon be here and Rollison did not want that
until he had talked to Alicia McGee.

Unless she had fled too.

He shivered as he drew the curtains and went across
and put three logs on to the embers, now glowing red.
Flames blazed as he straightened the pile of logs and the
fire irons. As he straightened up, grunting at the pain in
his back, Alicia McGee remarked from the door :

"How very domesticated."

He turned, to see her coming in with a laden tray—
coffee, milk, cheese, biscuits. He did not speak until she
had placed these on a table by the side of her chair.

"We both appear to be domesticated," he retorted.

"Ah, but you expect it from a woman."

"I'm not at all sure that I know what to expect from
you," Rollison retorted. "Is Jolly alive?"

Uttering the question actually hurt. He sensed that
she would tell the truth; that if Jolly were dead he would
soon know. The possibility created a fear and a tension
as great as he had ever known. He tried to relax his
features but they were stiff and set, and he had no doubt
at all that his feelings showed in his eyes.

If Jolly were dead he was quite capable of doing
murder.

She answered, very softly : "Yes. He is alive."

"If you are fooling me—" he said in a grating voice.

"I am not fooling you," she assured him. "I think that
had it been left to Michael, your man might have been
dead. Have you heard that his clothes were left by the
river at Chelsea Steps?"

She was uncanny in her knowledge; and almost as
uncanny in her ability to use a situation to anger, frighten

or to soothe.

"Yes," he said.

"That was Michael's bright idea. To take Jolly's clothes and make it look as if he had committed suicide."

"It doesn't seem a very bright idea to me. Where is Jolly?"

"It wasn't bright. You have no doubt noticed that Michael panics quite easily."

"Where is Jolly?" repeated Rollison, in a cold voice.

"He has been extremely good in some ways—an excellent cuckoo." She smiled winsomely. "I don't mean Jolly! It was entirely Michael's idea to lure Jolly from your flat. Michael telephoned the flat and said he must talk to you urgently, Jolly refused to wake you, but agreed to hear Michael out if he went round to your flat. Jolly opened the door and Michael with a companion overpowered him and carried him away. Michael was anxious, of course, to find out what you knew about my daughters."

It was so simple, now that it was explained; painfully simple.

"I understand that to spread confusion Michael left some lipstick smears on Jolly's pillow, when he went to get your man's clothes. Does it feel strange that you slept through all this, Mr. Rollison?"

"Strange," Rollison agreed. "But quite easy to understand. I was most intrigued."

"And apprehensive?"

"Not so apprehensive then as you should be now if you don't tell me where Jolly is," Rollison said, tautly.

"I will soon. I *do* know." She showed no sign of anxiety or fear. "I will gladly do a deal with you for Jolly." She moved again and began to pour out the coffee. The flames now leaping from the logs gave her a fine colour and the sharpness of her features actually took on a Mephistophelian look. "Sugar?"

Rollison said: "I will give you one more opportunity

to tell me where Jolly is. If you don't take it—". He paused as she straightened up, a cup and saucer in one hand and the silver coffee-pot in the other. Her smile was positively wicked; attractively wicked. "I shall send for the police."

Her smile dropped away.

"But I thought you preferred to act on your own?"

"Only when it will get quicker results."

"And if the police come here—"

"I shall tell them that you have been a party to murder and kidnapping. I shall show them the telephone from which the call to Superintendent Grice was made." He moved towards the telephone, ignoring the proffered coffee, and bent down for the receiver. His back seemed to break in two, but he showed no sign of pain. "You will find me easier to deal with than the police, and you have thirty seconds in which to make up your mind."

She looked at him for what must have been twenty of those thirty seconds. Then she shook her head, and put her coffee to her lips. She drank more than he expected but the truth did not dawn on him even as she lowered the cup.

"I need much more time than that," she said. "It isn't simply that I don't respond to any kind of threats, Mr. Rollison—I don't, of course, any more than you do. It is simply that I must think the situation out. While I have always been distrustful of Michael, I didn't expect to lose him so quickly!" When Rollison moved towards her, in truth not knowing what to do, she raised her cup to her lips again and finished the coffee. "I should warn you that he may think it wise to kill Jolly, who has no doubt learned a great deal."

Rollison stood very close to her.

"Where is Jolly? If Gogarty kills him it will be as much your fault as his."

She said: "Not as much, surely." She stifled a yawn, which he put down to affectation: as if she were playing with him cat and mouse. "Certainly I would never be blamed." She yawned again; and swayed.

That was the moment when Rollison realised how she had fooled him. That she had taken a drug in the coffee to put herself to sleep. He snatched the cup, or it would have fallen. She swayed against him and the saucer fell on to the carpet. On the instant she became a dead weight, and near terror raged inside him, as well as bitter self-reproach. He eased her into the big armchair and let her drop back. Her whole body was so slack and floppy, and he did not think there was any hope that she was pretending. He raised her right eyelid, and saw the pin-point pupil and knew that she had taken morphia; she might even have taken it before coming back into the room.

What the hell did that matter?

What could he do?

How right was she that Gogarty would decide that he must murder Jolly? The 'why' didn't matter . . .

Or was he wrong about that?

What could Jolly have found out to harm either Gogarty or Alicia McGee? And where could he have used the knowledge?

Where was Jolly?

Rollison looked at the unconscious woman. Her head slumped on her chest, and, even helpless, she looked as handsome as an eagle.

Eagle. Angel. *Angel!*

Where the hell was Jolly?

If Gogarty were going to kill him he could be followed to wherever Jolly was hidden.

Ah!

For the first time since he had realised how the woman had fooled him, Rollison felt a slight easing of tension. He began to move towards the telephone, picked it up and dialled 1212; almost immediately a voice answered.

"Is Superintendent Grice in?" He could not possibly know how strident he sounded.

"Just a moment, sir." The ensuing pause was only momentary. "He's on his way, sir, I can connect you to his car. Hold on, please." This time the pause was longer, but as Rollison tapped his foot with increasing impatience, first a squawk of atmospherics and then Grice came on the line.

"Bill," Rollison said, "the man you heard talking was Michael Gogarty, the P.R.O. of McGee's Soups. And he—"

"We've had a call in from the *Echo* about him," Grice interrupted. "He tried to run down one of their reporters near Mansell Square. Rolly—"

"He may be on his way to kill Jolly," Rollison sliced across Grice's words. "I don't know where."

"Wherever he is, we'll find him," Grice said. "What about you? Where are you?" He paused, then added: "What are you going to do?"

"I wish I knew," Rollison said, harsh in bitterness, and he hung up on Grice as he began to say: "Where are you? Rolly, don't take any more chances . . ."

Rollison stood for at least a minute, looking at Alicia McGee. At last, he turned away and began to search the room. There was a sixteenth-century French escritoire in oyster-pattern walnut in a rich brown shade, polished as with love. This was of the kind with many concealed drawers and panels, the only piece of furniture which was likely to hold anything of importance. At the front, easy to find, were some letters, bills, invitations, bank statements and securities; he had the impression that these had been put out to study in the past few hours. They told him that she was an enormously wealthy woman in her own right, worth at least three million pounds in securities alone. The sense of tension and urgency for Jolly made it difficult to concentrate, but he knew that he might make some discovery of great importance here.

He pressed the sides and the handles of tiny drawers
and shelves, and suddenly a drawer opened from what
had seemed a solid side of figured walnut. Inside were
some account books and a book of addresses. His heart
began to beat faster. He put the book aside but there was
a marker inside, and it fell open to a page of entries.
Here were payments to a bank; sums paid out for
investments; a complete record of Alicia McGee's hold-
ings. He thumbed through it, noticing the regularity of
the entries, none of which was for less than a hundred
thousand pounds.

And a hundred thousand pounds was the ransom fee
demanded for Marie!

He looked back at the beginning; the first entry was in
the early 1950s—when the triplets had been one year old.
He could almost hear Mary telling him how often and
for how long these kidnappings and ransoms had been
going on; at least once a year, she received payments and
bought different shares, some in McGee's Soups but
mostly in independent companies. She had large blocks in
Imperial Chemical Industries, B.P. Shell Oil, a host of
highly profitable stocks. Rollison folded the book, suddenly,
and pushed it into a side pocket of his jacket; the fit was
so tight that it would never fall out.

Hurriedly, he thumbed through the address book.

As far as he could see these were private addresses, but
why should anyone keep a day-to-day address book locked
away in a secret drawer? He began to study it more
closely, and discovered that most of the entries were
women—and that not all of them had a telephone
number. A hazy possibility entered his mind : that these
were the names and addresses of Rupert McGee's para-
mours. He turned to the W's : and on a second page, in
the middle of seven entries was *Edith White*.

There was only one mark against this entry, apart from
the address—71 Tenby Street, Whitechapel, E.1. And

that was 1969. There were dates against the other addresses, too—and no shadow of doubt that this was a comprehensive list of her husband's *affaires*. The range of addresses was quite remarkable : from Whitechapel to Whitehall, East Ham to Mayfair, Chelsea to Croydon, Fulham to Hampstead. All were in or near the London Metropolitan area and Rollison began to look for the number Whitechapel 43222, but did not find it.

He searched for men's addresses.

Here and there was one : *Elliot, George and Ethel, Flat 4c, 36 Giss Street, Fulham, S.W.6. Tel: Fulham 82135.* There was another : *Kidd, Patrick, Staff Flat, McGee Plant, Wapping—Whitechapel 43222.*

There was the number !

And Patrick Kidd, now under arrest and awaiting trial for at least one murder, had actually lived at the huge modern McGee factory where Rollison had been earlier tonight, and outside which he had met Edie White. Rollison put the address book down and turned to the telephone. Would anyone be at the flat? Would the police now be in possession? The only way to find out quickly was to telephone again. He dialled the number and stood waiting. His back ached when he stood for long, he had certainly put it out in that fall which had been so nearly onto the fire. The *brr-brr, brr-brr* of the ringing sound went on and on. If the police were there they would have answered by now. *Brr-brr, brr-brr.* He replaced the receiver slowly. He could go there, hoping to be ahead of the police, but would it serve any purpose?

He must find Jolly.

It was possible that Gogarty was under arrest by now, as possible that Gogarty had reached Jolly already. Tiredness was catching up on him. It must be past one o'clock, Physical weariness after the tension, the emotional strain and the pain, combined to exhaust him. Had to wake himself up ! He needed a drink. He picked up a bottle of whisky, poured himself a whisky and soda, and drank nearly as quickly as Alicia McGee had drunk the coffee. Slowly, the whisky began to affect him; weariness seemed to fade and his mind seemed to move more quickly. Illusion, he warned himself. He had another drink and dialled Whitechapel 43222 again, not so much hopeful as determined not to lose a chance of any kind.

"Brrr-brrr, brrr-brrr. brrr-brrr." It was no use, no one was at the other end of the line. *"Brrr-brrr."* He began to lower the receiver, when suddenly there was a *brrr-ach."* So someone *was* there! He put the receiver to his ear again but heard nothing except line noises, and a kind of grunting. Grunting?

"Hallo," he said sharply. "Hallo."

The grunting sound continued but there was no spoken response. Why? Who would answer the call and then not speak?

"Hallo!" he cried. "Are you there?"

A man said: *"Hol-on-plea. Hol-on-plea."*

Hold on, please? Was that what he was trying to say? The voice was hoarse, the words uttered as if with a great effort. *"Hold on, please."* He held on, chafing with impatience, until suddenly the man spoke again. This time his voice was clearer and Rollison knew on the instant who it was.

He had traced Jolly!

CHAPTER XVIII

The Hiding Place

"Is—*is* that you, sir?" Jolly asked, in an echoing voice. "Can it be?"

"Yes, Jolly," Rollison said, compelling himself to speak calmly. "How are you?"

"I—I'm all right, sir. I was—gagged." So that explained the grunting and the delay. "I managed—managed to—get the gag loose."

"Are you tied up?"

"Yes—yes, sir."

"I'll come for you, at once," Rollison said.

"I—I don't know where I am, sir," Jolly said, apologetically.

"I do," Rollison said.

"You—you do, sir?" Now Jolly's voice sounded both incredulous and enormously relieved. "Then where am I?"

"In a flat at McGee's soup factory," stated Rollison.

"That *would* explain certain things." Jolly was talking much more freely. "Sir, I can—"

"Just sit tight," Rollison said. "I won't be long."

"Sir!" exclaimed Jolly with such urgency that Rollison did not hang up at once. "Sir—they said they would kill you. Please—please send the police. Don't take risks for me, I beg you."

"Who said they would kill me?" asked Rollison.

"There—there were several men here only an hour ago," Jolly said. "Someone telephoned—someone named

Gogarty, I believe. He told them to get out, said the police might raid the flat. They—they all said they would kill you if you came anywhere near. If they're in the factory, they could be anywhere. The only safe way is to send the police. I *beg* you not to risk your own life."

"Jolly," Rollison said. "I won't come alone."

"I beg you not to, sir," Jolly said, and then in a different tone of voice, one which betrayed how despairing he felt: "Please—please don't be too long, sir. I haven't—haven't had anything to eat or drink since they brought me here."

"Jolly," Rollison said, "we'll be there before you can say 'knife'."

He rang off, seething; but he had no doubt at all what he had to do. He banged the receiver up and down until the 'ready' sound came again, and then dialled Bill Ebbutt's number. This time the ringing sound seemed to go on forever, he couldn't wait.

At last, Ebbutt's wheezy voice sounded.

"Who's that?"

"Bill," Rollison said. "Jolly is in the caretaker's flat at McGee's factory. There are probably several men waiting there as a kind of reception party for any rescue act. How many men can you get over to the flat in twenty minutes, say?"

All the time Ebbutt's wheezes came bubbling over the line, and almost before Rollison finished be burst out:

"A dozen enough?"

"Should be," Rollison conceded.

"Where—where shall I meet you, Mr. R?" That was better! No more formal Mr. Rollison.

"Let's say the Wapping High Street side."

"Okay."

"Have Mick Carter, Tiger Simms and John Sharples there," Rollison said. "We'll probably need them all."

"Okay!" cried Ebbutt, with a lift of elation, and then called: "Don't go, Mr. R! That telephone number, White-chapel something, Lenny the Link remembered. Once or twice he's had to call Gogarty, the P.R.O. of McGee's, at that number. Gogarty was up to something—don't ask me what!"

"I'll see you at the factory," Rollison said. He had no idea why Ebbutt had turned against him, but that was no longer urgent, and sooner or later he would be told.

He put down the receiver, and bent over the fireplace, picked up a short poker and slipped it into his waistband, where it did not hamper his movements. Quickly, he strode to the door. It seemed an age since he had come in here; an age since he had stood listening to Gogarty and Alicia McGee.

The light was still on in the passage.

He took out the key, opened the passage door and looked onto the dimly-lit landing. There was no sound. He went out, and swiftly but quietly downstairs. Crossing the hall, he saw that the front door was bolted and chained; and he also saw a switch built into the wall, which probably controlled the burglar alarm. A wire was chased into the door frame, he could make out where the paint was uneven. He turned the switch upwards, and nothing happened. He drew top and bottom bolts and unfastened the chain, opened the door and this time clenched his teeth and hunched his body against the biting cold. He closed the door behind him, and went as quickly as he could to the street. His back ached more than hurt, but when at last he bent to get into a taxi, he felt a stab as if he were breaking in two.

"McGee's factory, Wapping High Street," he told the driver.

"Okay, mate." The driver obviously judged him from the clothes he was wearing; Edie White's father's clothes. He leaned back in comparative comfort, and dared to close his eyes. There was absolutely nothing else he could do, and in the fifteen minutes or so that the journey would take, he could actually doze. And he dozed as they went through silent Knightsbridge with a few shop fronts lighted, through near-deserted Piccadilly and the wholly deserted Strand, Fleet Street, Bank and the City. There was some life at Aldgate, for some of the wholesale meat markets had night shifts, and not far off the lights at the docks showed, and the jangling noises of cranes and winches sounded clearly.

The rumbling of the taxi's wheels over the cobbles woke him; and he was wide awake as the driver turned into the approach road where he had been engulfed by workers earlier in the day : no, yesterday!

The lights, including the floodlights, were full on: obviously there was a night shift working; this was now an oasis of brightness in the mist of the dark streets and the high walls. Just beyond the big gates was a small building, obviously where the gate-keepers worked during the day. This was in darkness.

And somewhere inside was Jolly.

There was no sign yet of Bill Ebbutt and his men, but they certainly wouldn't be long. No one at all was in sight. There was a little clocking-in house, on the right of the main gates, but no one was inside it and although it was caught in the floodlights, no inside lights were on. One or two cars passed, tyres rumbling on the cobbles. Every time one approached, Rollison turned hopefully, waiting for it to slow down.

None did.

Why not? What was delaying Ebbutt? It must be half-an-hour since they had talked on the telephone, and the Blue Dog was only five minutes away by car. It could be walked, using the lanes and alleys, in less than twenty minutes.

Could anything have happened to Ebbutt?

Rollison turned restlessly, looked up at the iron railings and weighed the chances of climbing over. Were they electrified? Would a food factory so protect itself? Wouldn't a normal security force be enough—patrols with dogs, perhaps, or even in small cars. The floodlighting in itself was a form of protection.

He heard a car approaching, and waited in a patch of shadow with a mixture of eagerness and apprehension. This time it did slow down, and soon a car turned off the main road into this wide driveway. A man was at the wheel and there were at least three others with him. It didn't look like Ebbutt and it certainly wasn't Ebbutt's old T-Model Ford, in which he took such pride. This was a modern car, bigger than most. It pulled up close to the gates, and Rollison felt a flood of relief as he saw Benbow, and he moved out of the shadows.

Benbow got out of the car.

"Hallo, Mr. R," he said. "Been waiting long?"

"Longer than I expected to," Rollison said. "Where's Bill?"

"Believe it or not, just as he was going to leave he had a bit of trouble with his car," answered Benbow. He looked huge and had a fearsomely piratical manner. "He'll soon catch up. I brought back Carter and Johnny Sharples with me." The man who could break open a safe more easily than anyone in London, and the cat burglar who could climb virtually any wall, came out of the car.

"Mr. R," Carter said.

"How's it go, Toff?" asked Sharples.

"Cut the cackle," Benbow ordered, "and take a look at that lock."

Sharples, a short man, even shorter than Carter, who was small enough, unfastened a rope from his waist and tossed it over the gate. He obviously had not the slightest fear of being electrocuted. The rope looped over a spike and with remarkable agility and speed he climbed up it, over, and dropped down. He landed light as a cat, and moved towards the lock of the gates, so that he stood on one side and Carter stood on the other.

"How does it look?" asked Carter.

"Easy from the side," answered Sharples. "I can fix it." Metal touched metal for a moment, and there was a grating sound as he busied himself with a skeleton key. Suddenly there was a clatter, and he said: "Okay." He pulled and Carter pushed at the heavy gate, which opened easily on oiled hinges.

"In we go," said Benbow.

Rollison, Benbow and a third man went in. Sharples closed the gates, let them slip and made them clang.

"Quiet!" breathed Benbow.

"Why, no one—" Sharples began, and then broke off.

Rollison, very close to the main lock, looked at it briefly but searchingly. He saw a bolt fixed to a padlock. He saw that the bolt wasn't fully home. He looked at the ladder, tossed up there as if with long practice. He recalled Sharples: "Why, no one—" and the abrupt finish to the sentence, obviously at a glare from Benbow. He recalled his astonishment that Benbow, not Ebbutt, had turned up. He could well believe that the Model-T Ford might break down but it was almost impossible to believe that Ebbutt would allow someone else to take his place.

All of these things crowded one another in his mind, and he knew the truth at last; almost as soon as he began to think.

Benbow wasn't trustworthy; nor were those with him.

Three of the five men whom Ebbutt had recommended were unreliable, among them the powerful Benbow and the man whom he now knew to be Tiger Simms; Tiger was a well-known strong-arm man.

What were they up to? What on earth had gone wrong?

"Come on, Mr. R," Benbow said, impatiently. "Thought you told Bill that Jolly was here."

"He's in the caretaker's flat," Rollison answered, very slowly.

"So let's go get him."

"Do you know where the flat is?" Rollison asked.

"As well as I know the galley in the barge," Benbow answered roundly. "It's above the wages office. We've all worked here, some time or other. Haven't we, boys?"

There was a muted chorus of agreement. "Just follow me."

"Supposing the place is guarded?" Rollison demurred.

"That's what we're here for, isn't it? To take care of anyone who tries to stop us."

Benbow took Rollison's right arm as he spoke. He did not grip tightly enough to hurt but his hold was very firm. He was one of the most powerful men Rollison knew, and he was crowding Rollison. Sharples and Tiger Simms were close behind, as if to make sure Rollison could not turn and run.

"How did you find out Jolly was here?" asked Benbow.

"I telephoned," replied Rollison. He did not want to warn them that he knew that there was something badly wrong, and he spoke quite calmly.

"You mean he *answered?*" exclaimed Benbow, unbelievingly.

"He'd been gagged for hours but slipped the gag."

"He's nearly as good as you, Toff," Sharples said from close to Rollison's left shoulder.

"He's a lot better than I shall ever be," Rollison said.

"Mock modesty," Sharples jeered. "That's what you say."

"That's enough," Benbow interrupted. "You always did talk too much, Johnny. Any idea what all the trouble is about, Toff?"

Toff. Mr. Rollison. 'Mr. R' was beginning to fade.

"Not yet," Rollison said. "Except—"

The pressure from Benbow's fingers grew stronger; slowly but perceptibly stronger. Menacingly?

"Except what?" Benbow demanded.

"McGee's public relations man, Gogarty, is involved."

"In what?" demanded Benbow.

"Among other things, kidnapping."

"What other things?" Benbow demanded, and now his grip was painful, and he actually seemed to push Rollison.

Rollinson eased his arm. For a moment he thought the

other would stop him from getting free, but suddenly the grip relaxed, although only slightly.

They had crossed the main approach to the factory along a path where there was little light, but now they were at the end of the path and another two steps would take them into bright light. All of them paused. Only about fifty feet away was a two-storey building, rather like an annexe to the factory. All of the lights were out but the floodlights showed that this was really a small house.

Was Jolly in there?

"What other things, Toff?" Benbow repeated, and there was not even lingering doubt of the menace in his voice.

"Murder," Rollison answered.

"Whose murder?"

"A couple named Elliot, for a start," Rollison said. His mind was racing ahead of his words; what could he do? "Is that the place where Jolly is held?"

"That's it. The ground floor's the wages office, it's got special protection when there's money in it," Benbow told him. "The flat is above." There was a pause and then Benbow added with a sneer: "As if you didn't know."

Rollison said simply: "I've never been here before."

"Don't give me that," said Benbow. "You've been taking chances with Jolly from the first, you bloody Toff."

Benbow was wrong but it would take evidence, not words, to convince him, and no evidence was at hand. At least his certainty gave Rollison a glimmering of the reason for Ebbutt's period of hostility. If Benbow believed this of him then he, Benbow, must surely have near-convincing proof. But it didn't matter where he had it or what it was; what mattered was to outwit Benbow now.

"Are you sure that's the place?" Rollison asked as if he was far from convinced.

"That's it," insisted Sharples, *sotto voce*. "Jolly's little hide-out."

'Hide-out' was a sneer. It was deliberately mis-used, of course, and there was no longer any doubt that Sharples was riding him; that very soon these men would show their hand. Rollison appeared to notice nothing, was aware of Benbow's pressure increasing again before saying:

"Don't ask me what it's all about. I'm here to find Jolly. I don't care what the McGees or Gogarty or anyone else has been doing, all I want is Jolly. So let's go." If he resisted, if he let Benbow see his suspicions were aroused he might not have a chance to get the upper hand.

He actually led the way into the lighted patch; anyone glancing this way could see them, but getting across only took seconds. Rollison reached the shadows in a porch overlooking the front door, and as he did so he swivelled round, pulled the pistol from his pocket and the poker from his waistband, and said softly:

"What shall it be, Benbow? A bullet in the heart or a slap with a poker on the back of the neck?"

All four stood like men in a trance; all four, facing him, were within arm's reach. Any one of them could fling himself forward and be shot—but if two took the risk at the same moment, there would be little hope for him.

And none of these men was a coward.

CHAPTER XIX

Danger

The main danger would come from Benbow. Rollison sensed that from the way the man shifted his position onto his toes, so as to leap forward; and the way his chin thrust forward. Tiger was ready, too, already on the balls of his feet. If Rollison had a chance, it was now.

He fired the little pistol at Benbow's right shoulder. Flash, report, gasp, all seemed to come at the same moment. Benbow rocked backwards. Tiger dropped back on his heels. Rollison held the gun poised, covering Sharples. The echoes of the shot died away and no one called out, no one else approached.

"Turn round," Rollison ordered.

None of them moved.

"Turn round," repeated Rollison.

Sharples leapt at him, eyes glinting in the floodlights. Rollison whipped out the poker and struck him on the side of the head. There was a crack of sound and a gasp as the man staggered sideways. He fell gradually to his knees, then sprawled on the grass.

"Mick," Rollison said to Carter, "open the door for me."

Mick hesitated, looking at Benbow, who was pressing his left palm against the wound in his shoulder. Tiger Simms was holding back, perhaps scared now; yet he was the strong-arm man of the party.

"Micky," Rollison called, very softly, "I can do it

myself but I'd have to crack your skull first."

Benbow grunted: "Open it."

Rollison moved to one side as Mick Carter came forward and bent over the door. He really was an expert. Metal scraped on metal, and there was a click, before Mick pushed the door open. Rollison waved him away. He backed closer to Benbow and Tiger Simms. Sharples, a heap on the ground, hadn't moved. Rollison went towards the door, keeping them covered, and slipped inside. Locking the door on them wouldn't help. He put on a light, and fluorescent strip flickered, crackled and then spread a false daylight. There were bolts; and by the side of the door a burglar alarm switch. He pressed it down. He saw Mick Carter's lips move; the man was swearing viciously.

Now Rollison was on his own, absolutely on his own. He backed across the room. It was a gate-house and time-keeping office, really, very bare, very clean-looking. There was a door in the wall behind him, and he opened it. The men outside were moving away; certainly they weren't planning an immediate counter-attack, but they might be going for help.

He stepped into a passage, where there was near-darkness, groped for and found a light switch; another fluorescent strip came on. This room had only heating units and some wooden chairs, as well as doorways to a kitchen, a bathroom, and a W.C. A flight of stairs loomed on the right and Rollison went up them. They were covered with haircord carpet, soft and silent underfoot. At the top of the stairs was a landing lit only by the light from below, but Rollison found another fluorescent strip.

Now he was in the flat; and there were several doors leading off on one side, one room obviously on top of the big room below. He stood very still and called without raising his voice:

"Jolly."

There was no response, so he raised his voice a little.

"Jolly!"

Almost at once there came an answering call, excited, eager : "Is that you, sir?"

He *had* found Jolly!

He felt the shock of relief run through his body, along his nerves. He stood for a few seconds, utterly still, and then he and Jolly called at the same moment.

"Is that you, sir?" Now Jolly was anxious.

"Which room are you in?" Rollison called. "Tap at the door."

After a pause, a tap came from the middle of three rooms on the left, opposite the biggest room over the office. He stepped towards it.

"All right!" He looked at the lock and saw the key in it, and then turned it slowly and pushed, adding : "Stand back a little."

Slowly, the door opened; and only a few feet away from the door crouched Jolly. His hands were tied behind him, and there was a loop of rope at his ankles. He looked pale and sick, and his eyes were huge and red-rimmed. The patches under them were very dark. But he was smiling. And as Rollison moved towards him, more affected than he could hope to say, Jolly breathed :

"It—it's very good to see you, sir."

"Good is the word," Rollison said gruffly. He went behind Jolly, and saw the red rawness at the bony wrists where Jolly had tried to free himself. He took out his penknife and cut through the rope, easing the pressure as much as he could. The rope fell, and Jolly staggered. Rollison supported him towards a bed in a corner, and helped him onto it.

He had never seen tears in Jolly's eyes before.

"Soon have you out," he said, cutting the looser ropes at the ankles. He rested a hand lightly on Jolly's shoulder. "I'll get you something."

"Sir," Jolly said, in a gasping way. "We—" He broke off.

"What is it, Jolly?"

"They'll come for us, sir. They won't—won't let us out."

"I'll be back in a moment. You try to rest," Rollison urged.

". . . . I know too much," Jolly managed to say.

"Two minutes," Rollison said.

He picked up the telephone, but it was dead; so there was not a hope of calling for help. At least he'd made the call to Jolly.

What did Jolly know? Why was he so sure it would bring 'them' back. Whom did he mean by 'they'? The questions chased one another through Rollison's mind as he found a kitchen, with a refrigerator, in it some milk, fresh bread and butter. He put them on a tray with a glass, and went back; he couldn't have been gone more than three minutes. Jolly was sitting up in the bed and massaging his ankles; his wrists were blood raw. Rollison poured out cold milk, and Jolly's hand quivered as he tried to hold the glass.

"Let me," said Rollison.

He put a hand to his man's back and the glass to his lips. Jolly sipped; and then drank, greedily, until the glass was nearly empty. Rollison put it back on the tray, went into a bathroom leading off the bedroom, ran warm water and poured a little of an antiseptic in it, soaked and wrung out a towel. He took this to Jolly, and gently bathed the raw wrists.

"Ready for another drink?"

"If—if we are to get away, we must go now," Jolly urged.

"Soon, I promise you. Feel better?"

"It's very soothing, sir. I—I know what it is all about." Every word he uttered was a palpable effort.

"Must you tell me now?" Rollison almost pleaded. He was so desperate to know, as desperate to start on his way out of here. Benbow and the others would be there to stop him one way, of course. But did Jolly mean Benbow and his men? "If we're to get out—"

"There is the back way, sir."

"Through the wages office?"

"Yes—isn't that how you got in?" Jolly sounded certain.

"Yes—and it's not how we'll get out."

Jolly said in a helpless voice : "There isn't any other way, sir."

"There must be."

"There isn't," Jolly insisted. "This annexe is cut off from the main building by electronically controlled steel doors, like the fireproof doors on a ship. The men went out that way. The control is from the other side. There simply isn't another way out except the way you came in, sir. What—what kind of risk is involved by going out the way you came in?"

"Too big a risk to take," Rollison said, in a flat voice; but he knew it might have to be taken.

There was a pause which seemed to last for a long time before Jolly spoke again, in a voice and a manner which seemed to come out of the past. A firm voice; a voice of authority, brooking no denial.

"Master Richard, we must leave by that exit, and at once. This particular part of the premises will be destroyed, by explosives, in less than ten minutes. I hoped to get away without worrying you, but obviously you are in one of your obdurate moods."

Rollison momentarily gaped.

And then, helplessly, he laughed; and the laughter seemed to convulse him. There was Jolly, hardly capable of walking; he, himself, with a back so strained that he could hardly move without pain; the certainty that Benbow and the others were waiting for them outside; and the almost incredible fact that Jolly had withheld this devastating information until the very last moment.

"Master Richard!" Jolly actually raised his voice.

"Yes," Rollison said. "Yes, I know. Benbow and some of his friends will be waiting for us, though."

"We really haven't time to talk," breathed Jolly. "We must go."

Rollison said again : "Yes."

He had the pistol with four—or was it three?—bullets left in it. He checked, to find three. He had the poker. And he had Jolly. He eased his man off the bed. The full force of Jolly's information struck home at last : this place was to be blown up by a time bomb. *Why?* As he supported Jolly his own back almost gave way but his mind was working.

"Just this annexe, Jolly?"

"Yes, sir."

"Who put the bomb there and where is it?"

"The man Gogarty, sir. I really have no idea where."

"Jolly, we have to find it."

Jolly was silent for an anguished moment, and then said : "Oh, dear God." And loudly : "It was intended to kill me, sir, so that I couldn't talk."

"Nonsense," Rollison said, briskly. "They could have killed you a dozen different ways. They want the place blown up. Do you know if there's a cellar?"

"I—I've no idea, sir."

"I'll go down and see what I can find," Rollison said. "You come as quickly as you can. What time do you say it's supposed to blow up?"

"At one-thirty, and it is one-twenty now," Jolly answered. He was standing without help, and there was some colour in his cheeks. "Sir—it isn't worth dying for. Whatever it is, it's not worth that."

"If I don't find it I'll give myself two minutes to get clear. You stay by the door but out of sight of anyone watching." He gripped Jolly's shoulder for a moment before going out of the room and down the stairs. He had seen no sign of a cellar, but there was a passage alongside the stairs. He saw a door which he hadn't noticed before, marked *Staff Only*. He rounded the iron rail of the staircase and pushed at this.

It opened to reveal another set of stone stairs.

There was a switch at the top and he pressed it. Light flooded the steps and the cellar beyond. Even as he went down, he thought he heard a ticking sound; or was that imagination heightened by what Jolly had told him? He stood still at the foot of the stairs, his heart-beats loud in his ears; almost suffocating. There *was* a *tick-tick-tick*, and it seemed to be coming from his right, beyond rows and rows of green metal filing cabinets.

He moved slowly towards the sound.

There must be forty cabinets here, standing in lines. There was also a bench and some padded stools, but nothing else : this was just a filing room.

And the clock, the ticking time bomb, must be in one of the filing cabinets.

He reached the nearest, and pulled at the top drawer. *It was locked*. There was a keyhole at the top right hand corner of this and the other cabinets in sight; a single lock controlled all four drawers. The locks were Yale. There was no possible way of forcing forty locks in, say seven minutes; even Mick Carter would not have a hope.

What the devil was he thinking about? He could locate it by listening.

The ticking was coming from his right. He walked along the passageway between two rows of filing cabinets, on tiptoe. The sound was getting louder. He paused at one cabinet, and placed his ear close to it : no sound came from any of its drawers. He reached the next, which was also silent, but from the third came a loud *tick-tick-tick*. He went down on one knee and pressed his ear against each drawer.

It was in the bottom one.

Slowly, he straightened up, grunting at the stabbing pain in his back. He did not notice Jolly, now at the foot of the stairs. He had one tool which might force this lock,

a knife blade or very pliant steel which could be shaped
by pressure to enter any lock. He opened his knife, then
heard a sound, and started up.

Jolly was halfway towards him.

"I thought I told you to wait by the door," Rollison
said sharply.

"Can—can I help, sir?"

"I've found the infernal machine," Rollison said.
"What's the time?"

"There are five minutes to go, sir."

"Plenty," Rollison declared. He pushed the end of the
blade between the barrel of the lock and the fitting on
the cabinet, and gradually the steel took on the shape of
the barrel. It seemed to take an age. "Hear it?" asked
Rollison. Jolly didn't answer. Rollison pushed harder but
with infinite care, and the blade began to disappear.

Suddenly, there was a sharp click.

"Got it!" gasped Rollison. He bent down and pulled
at the handle of the bottom drawer very, very slowly.

It opened : he *had* forced the lock.

He pulled it wider open, and as he did so Jolly's
blood-reddened hands appeared, Jolly put both hands
inside the drawer and clutched, and brought out a box.
The ticking coming from it was much louder.

"Upstairs," Rollison said. "We can't hope to dismantle
it. Let me—"

"I can manage, sir." Jolly now hugged the infernal
machine to his chest. *Tick-tick-tick* it went, like a song.
He lengthened his stride, reached the stairs and started
up. Rollison had to grip the handrail, he could not have
gone up as steadily as Jolly. Jolly reached the top. There
couldn't be more than two or two and a half minutes to
go. Rollison passed Jolly into the main office. There was
no time for anything but direct action, and if there was
an attack from outside, then they were finished. He
opened the door wide, and shouted :

"Get away! There's a time bomb. Get away!"

No one answered.

But he saw men and cars beyond the gates. He saw men climbing the gates. He bellowed again but there was no answer from nearby. He held the door wide open and Jolly went past, and that awful *tick-tick-tick* went on.

"Put it close to the wall," Rollison said hoarsely. The wall was only a few yards away, clear in the floodlights. Jolly lowered it. *Tick-tick-tick.* He placed the box on the ground, and Rollison breathed : "*Run.*" They couldn't really run, they could only hobble, but fear lent desperation and insulation against pain. If the explosion were coming, it would come any moment. They were on the other side of the wall. Men were running towards them from the gates which were wide open. "*Down!*" shouted Rollison at the top of his voice. "*Down!*"

He plunged forward and Jolly dived, too. As they hit the ground a roar came with deafening force and the blast struck them with cold fury, and lifted them and hurled them down; and debris from the wall and clods of earth from the ground thudded all about them.

CHAPTER XX

Deep Laid Plot

Rollison was aware first of faces, then of voices, then of faces. There was Bill Ebbutt and Bill Grice. Grice was doing most of the talking, a sharp-featured man whose face seemed very pale in the floodlights.

"He's all right—nothing is broken."

Rollison said in a husky voice: "Jolly."

"He's not hurt, just has a scratch or two, apart from his wrists. Like a drink of water?" Ebbutt on Rollison's other side, held a flask in a big, steady hand. Someone out of sight supported Rollison's back, and he held his breath, expecting pain: it didn't come. The water was ice-cold: nectar.

"More?"

"No—no thanks. Where are we?"

"In the gate-house," Grice answered. "We'll have you home very soon."

"Mr. R," Ebbutt said, wheezing less than usual, "I ought to be shot. I was a credulous idiot, that's what I was. Benbow fooled me proper. He was working with Gogarty and Alicia McGee—whatever made me think she was an angel!—to kill old Rupert and take over the company. I never knew, Mr. R—I trusted Benbow like I did the others, I never knew they'd been got at."

Rollison looked incredulously at Grice.

"Did *you* know this, Bill?"

"Gogarty's made a statement, and so has Benbow,"

Grice replied. "The gist of what Ebbutt is telling you is right."

"I got to get it off me mind," declared Ebbutt, "I got to tell you meself, and Mr. Grice said okay, go ahead." He gave a wheezy cough before going on : "First off, Benbow said he'd *seen* you kill the Elliots, and I thought you were so infuriated about Jolly you was quite capable of cutting their throats—but it meant you wasn't yourself, Mr. R. Then he said you'd paid him to look after two of the McGee girls, on his barge. *And* he said he'd heard you talking to a man who offered Jolly in exchange for the girls, and you wouldn't do the deal. That's what finally tipped me over, Mr. R—the thought of you putting those girls before Mr. Jolly."

"Benbow must have been very convincing," Rollison said mildly.

"Well, Sharples and another chap said they'd heard this, too—I just didn't know they'd been got at, Mr. R."

"Do you know why they'd been got at?" Rollison asked.

Ebbutt said: "I'm going to hand over to Mr. Grice now, but—strewth, I wish I could tell you how sorry I am! Even at the last I sent Benbow and his pals to you, to make sure you didn't get up to no funny business over Jolly. I want my head examined, that's the truth."

"It wasn't all your fault," Grice put in quietly. "I'd told him I was sure you'd gone berserk after Jolly's disappearance. And if you'd seen the blood in that room—" Grice broke off.

"Go on," Rollison said bleakly.

"I'll be as brief as I can," promised Grice. "We've got two of the girls from the barge, and the third's now with them at a flat in Knightsbridge. I've put together what Gogarty, Benbow and the girls have stated. First: Mrs. She and Gogarty had been steadily transferring shares to McGee finally decided she'd had enough of her husband. themselves, forging signatures—and he found out, so they planned to kill him."

"Then *he* found out and couldn't get out of England fast enough," put in Ebbutt.

"He had told his daughters and they could hardly believe it, and they wanted help—so they came to you. They—"

"Don't try to tell me the kidnapping of Mary was a hoax!" exclaimed Rollison.

"That was in deadly earnest," Grice answered. "Gogarty put the Elliots up to it. The idea was to scare the girls to silence about their father and his danger. Mary McGee says they were utterly confused, not wanting to betray their mother, yet wanting to help their father, and all they could think of was getting you involved."

"If they'd told me the truth—" began Rollison, only to break off. "What next, Bill?" he asked.

"Gogarty and Benbow sent Kidd to kill the Elliots, who could have given far too much away," Grice answered. "They are a cold-blooded, ruthless lot, Rolly. They hoped to be able to keep you out of the chase by kidnapping Jolly—did Gogarty telephone and warn you off?"

"Yes—but I didn't know it was Gogarty at the time," Rollison answered wryly.

"When that failed, they began to start to discredit you, and they had some major help when your fingerprints were found at the Giss Street apartments."

"What on?" asked Rollison. "I ought to be shot for leaving them."

"On a radiator," Grice answered. "There was just the one: obviously you'd been warming your hand." When Rollison made no comment but looked aghast, Grice continued: "There was another very misleading factor too. Nothing you could blame yourself about, this time."

"I suppose that's something," conceded Rollison, grudgingly. "What, Bill?"

"The Tidy youths who came to your flat," said Grice, "The one who was killed knew what was going on. His brother only knew he was coming with Patrick Kidd to kill you, and came to try to stop him. The dead one, Jimmy, could have named Kidd as the Elliots' murderer and Benbow as one of the men involved. When we had a report that you were seen talking to the dead man's girl-friend outside the factory, we thought you knew already, and were doing a deal with Benbow for Jolly." Grice went on.

"Well, well," said Rollison, and added almost irrele-vantly, "Poor Edie."

"Edie White, that's right," confirmed Grice. "What did you want from her?"

"Information she didn't have," Rollison answered quietly, and Grice was satisfied. "But she wasn't a happy person and she seemed to have a love-hate relationship with McGee's factory."

"So do most of the employees," Ebbutt interrupted. "Like I told you, Mr. R."

"You did indeed, Bill." Rollison looked straight into the eyes of the other Bill, Grice, and asked: "What was Benbow to get out of this?"

"One hundred thousand pounds, half of which he got in advance, plus anything he could take from the strong-room and safes after the explosion."

"And the real villain of the piece is Alicia McGee?" asked Rollison, almost unbelieving.

"Yes," Grice answered, "there doesn't seem any doubt of it at all. And yet—" He threw up his hands in bewilder-ment, puzzling the Toff. It was Ebbutt, who did not look puzzled but simply sad, who tried, uncertainly, to explain:

"She was tired of her husband wasting money on women, he spent fortunes on some of them—and she was sick of the way he treated some of the girl employees. And she wanted to make the factory a kind of co-operative, but Rupert wouldn't agree. She'd been getting money by fake kidnappings for a long time, then set her target much higher with Gogarty's help. Whether she would have put her plans into action, no one will ever know."

"Where is she?"

"In a police cell," Grice answered. "She's been charged with conspiracy to kidnap Jolly—" He looked at Jolly, who spread his hands out with a touch of humility, as if to say that in spite of everything he wished her well.

A few minutes later, with Jolly by his side, Rollison was in a police car. Twenty minutes later the car drew up outside 25 Gresham Terrace. He walked upstairs with little discomfort; whatever part of his back had been put out, the movement by the blast had put it right again. As they reached the landing the door opened. Rollison expected to see Rose Sapelli, but instead he saw the near-identical triplets.

There was Mary, very bright-eyed, her hair a little fluffier than the others.

There was Marie, perhaps half an inch taller, with her hair sleeker.

There was Maria, her lips set tightly and, although of the same age within minutes, looking perhaps a little older than the others. In her eyes was a look which might well be a pleading for forgiveness.

"Toff," said Mary, softly.

"*Dear* Toff," breathed Marie.

"Toff," said Maria, "haven't *you* ever behaved like an idiot and realised it when it was just too late?"

"Never too late," said Rollison. He spread his arms, and suddenly Mary and Marie were clutched in one, as it were, and as suddenly Rose appeared and was clutched, with Maria, in the other. Almost as if they had been rehearsing for weeks, they went a little tearfully into the big trophy room, where there was tea and coffee and drinks all waiting. Grice and Jolly brought up the rear, and each of the triplets took a moment off to go to Jolly, and shake his hand; only Mary kissed his cheek.

Then Jolly sat in one armchair, Rollison in another, and the triplets perched on pouffes in a half-circle about them and Rose began to pour coffee while Grice—almost a teetotaller—mixed himself a weak whisky-and-soda when the others had opted for coffee.

"Now," Rollison said, "the time has come for final explanations."

"Oh, Toff," said Mary. "I feel aw-aw-awful."

"I feel worse," said Marie and there were actually tears in her eyes.

"Nonsense," said Maria, in her firmest voice and with a stern expression. "We did what he would have done in the circumstances. Toff, we knew our father was in danger, we didn't know much else. I actually saw him off at London Airport—and when a police car stopped us for speeding I thought the police had come to arrest Daddy. I was terrified."

"And livid," murmured Rollison.

"I often get livid," Maria admitted. "Mother always says I have enough bad temper for all three of us, I'm a kind of balance to Mary and Marie's holier-than-thou-ishness." Her sisters smiled, but there was sadness in them. "What we didn't expect was Mother to strike so soon."

"You knew she was involved?" asked Rollison, marvelling.

"We feared she was," said Maria. "We knew that she and Daddy put on an act but they hated each other, really. I think I told you early on that we had a strange upbringing. A father with no conventional morals at all, a mother who saw us as dice in a game, rather than human beings. I hope that in view of everything, we've come out fairly well. At least, the other two have."

"M-M-Maria," declared Mary, "you're worth t-t-two of us."

"Nearly all three of us," murmured Marie.

"We wanted you to find out, and we told Mother that we were going to enlist you," breathed Mary.

"She kidnapped Jolly and fought back," marvelled Maria. "She's a remarkable woman, she really is."

There was such sadness in her voice; and there were

tears in Mary's and a hint of tears in Marie's eyes. Rose suddenly bustled into movement, with sugar and cream and a great variety of biscuits and for a while no one spoke.

At last Rollison said in a voice quite free from emotion:

"Then as I understand it, Rupert McGee, your father, can come back if he wishes to."

"He'll come back," Maria said, with a glint in her eyes. "And *we'll* find a way of making him turn over a lot of the shares to the workers—what Mummy's always wanted to do."

"I'll gladly put my money in!" cried Mary, and all of a sudden she looked happy.

"And mine! I have always wanted to model," said Marie, intently.

"I suggest we put in three-quarters of what we have to the common pool," said Maria. "I don't really think we need put everything in. After all we were always the pawns in the game. Don't you agree?" she demanded of the Toff, and the light of battle dawned in her eyes.

"I do," murmured Rollison.

Grice simply nodded, as if he felt quite overwhelmed.

Rollison made sure that Jolly was comfortably in bed, with Rose ministering, before leaving the apartment with Grice. They did not speak until they were in the street, where the night air was quite mild.

"Where are you going?" asked Grice.

"To see a girl in Tenby Street," Rollison answered. "Once the girl-friend of Patrick Kidd. I think she might be dreadfully upset when she knows he's been arrested. Do you know anything more about him?"

"Yes," answered Grice, briskly. "Patrick Kidd worked on barges, near the Arrow's mooring, and he was in a dinghy alongside and heard Benbow and Sharples plotting against you. So they cut him in. Young Jimmy Tidy hero-worshipped him and Kidd used him as a decoy to make you an easy target. And it would probably have come off if Fred Tidy hadn't tried to stop him. Fred is with an aunt, and he'll be all right."

"That's one good thing," said Rollison, with deep feeling.

He drove in the small car to Edie White's house, and found her still up, alone, and desolate; she had been told of Pat's arrest, and it hurt desperately; he had mattered so much more than she had allowed herself to admit. Rollison, deeply glad that he had gone to see her, let her cry for a while, and soon afterwards, took her to the Blue Dog, where Ebbutt's wife put her up for the night, so that she would not be alone.

The Toff drove back to Gresham Terrace, very tired, but lighter of heart than he had been since the first McGee triplet had telephoned him. When he went upstairs, Jolly was asleep and Rose dozing in an armchair. He sent her to the spare room and went to bed himself.

It was mid-morning before he woke, to find Rose by his side with morning tea.

"I've taken Mr. Jolly's in," she said. "He seems okay. I wouldn't have woke you but Mr. Grice is coming round in about an hour to clear up some odds and ends, he said. Oh—and there's a parcel. One of those triplets brought it."

She produced the parcel from the foot of the bed, and Rollison opened it, puzzled but eager. Very soon he saw that there were three small tins of McGee Soups inside, and between two of them, a card. He drew this out, and glanced down to see:

Please put these on your Trophy Wall.
Mary, Marie and Maria.

He began to chuckle, and Rose laughed, too, and Jolly came in his dressing-gown to share the joke.

VOTE FOR THE TOFF

by JOHN CREASEY

Elections ought to be peaceful affairs – but when they go wrong it's useful to have a Toff in the offing

Those who know him, those who have shared his lifelong devotion to helping the under-dog, know that Rollison is not joking.

But there are others who think that his desire to contest a Parliamentary election is just a playboy's whim, a passing fancy . . . which is not so.

And still others who react with vicious threats and brutal murder because they think his politicking is just a cover for a foray against a ring of drug-pushers . . . which is partly so.

Other TOFF titles in CORONET are listed over the page . . .

CORONET FOR CREASEY

THE TOFF SERIES

GIDEON, THE BARON and INSPECTOR WEST — ALSO IN CORONET
